Dragon Blood

Books 1 & 2

By

Élianne Adams

Cover Art by Fantasia Frog Designs

Paperback ISBN 978-1-988644-07-3

Deadly Whispers Series
Bump in the Night
Fallen Angel

Single Titles
Black Velvet
Burn Deep

Coming Soon!

Mates of the Citadel Series
Damon
Axton
Keilon

Releasing Her Dragon

Elianne Adams

http://elianneadams.com/

« CHAPTER 1 »

Dark indigo, nothing more than a wink in the moonlight, drew Stella's attention, and then it was gone. *You're not getting away from me, not this time.* When she had last given chase, she'd been too eager, too desperate, and he had given her the slip—again.

The forest whispered to her, soothing her with the soft rustling of leaves, giving her the courage to do what she was about to do even though inside, she trembled. If he wanted nothing to do with her, then she'd deliver her speech and have him release her. Nothing difficult there, except, deep down, she yearned for him to want her as desperately as she wanted him, but she would hold her head up high and move on. What choice did she have? If she didn't mate—and soon—she would shift and never come back.

The only movement she allowed herself was the rise and fall of her chest. If he suspected she was near, caught her scent or heard the slightest sound, he would never reveal himself, and she couldn't take that chance.

She didn't need to see him to know he was near. Every nerve ending in her body tingled, vibrating with need. Soon she would know him, and one way or the other, she'd be free of the constant ache thrumming through her. The incessant need keeping her awake at night, tossing and turning as her body made demands she wasn't equipped to satisfy.

A thick flowery perfume drifted to her nose, drawing her gaze back to the clearing. The cloying scent clung to the breeze, as it wafted past. Was he meeting someone here in the woods? A woman? Heart pounding, she used every bit of hard-earned discipline she had to keep from leaping over the knoll hiding her from them.

The quiet of the night unnerved her, but it wasn't a surprise. Not a single creature dared draw the predator's attention, and there was no denying he was a predator. Even the scavengers lay in their holes, hoping he'd pass them by. Time stretched until she just couldn't sit still anymore. She had to see him. Had to see where that floral scent came from, because it sure wasn't from the forest's natural blossoms.

Taking care not to make the slightest sound, she lifted her torso from the moss-covered ground, uncaring that the damp earth clung to her curves. She wasn't there to entice him after all, only to find out who he was, and if she were lucky, talk to the man.

She'd never gotten this close. The perfume all but obliterated the scent Stella desperately sought. If she could just sniff him, she would know that this was the man meant for her. But what was a she-dragon to do? She couldn't very well walk up to strange men and start smelling them.

When she didn't see anything in the clearing ahead, she stretched further, tucking her legs beneath her. Her shoulders slumped, and she sighed. Had he given her the slip again? No, he couldn't have. Her blood still sang in her veins and her body still ached with neglect.

She had to be patient. A slight movement, nothing more than a shift, brought her attention to the tree line. His massive head tilted in her direction as he took in his surroundings. For such a huge beast, he blended well. Almost too well. No wonder it had been so hard to track him. His blue scales caught the shadows instead of standing out in the moonlight. Had she been a mere human, she could have walked right past and never known he was there.

The pointed end of his tail twitched in the grass, back and forth in quick, impatient jerks. Whatever he was doing, he wasn't happy about it.

"There you are. Have you been waiting long?" A soft feminine voice drifted up to her ears. The moment it did, Stella had to fight from leaping to get to the woman before she got anywhere near the dragon.

The rumble of his growl filtered through the brush, making her skin prickle with awareness.

His tail fanned the grass again.

"Come on, Brycen, get rid of the scales so we can talk." Stella couldn't see the woman's face, but if the childlike tone she'd laced the words with were any indication, she was pouting and batting her eyelashes at him. Nauseating.

The woman tossed her blond tresses over her shoulder and brought her hand up to his neck, sliding it down as though she had every right. Fury coursed through every part of her, and Stella had to grind her teeth to keep the growl from erupting from her throat.

A small puff of steam wafted from his nostrils, then with a shuddering sigh, he allowed the change to take him. The indigo scales shivered and shook, shrinking upon themselves until he took his human form. A spattering of scales covered his groin, leaving the rest bare for the woman's perusal. *Step out from the shadows. I need to see your face, Brycen.* At least now she knew his name. His identity had eluded her for far too long already, and she was done waiting for him to stop running. Because it was obvious, he wouldn't.

Stella held her breath. Just a couple of steps and the moonlight would give him away. With her better than average eyesight, she'd be able to see him and recognize him anywhere. Catching his scent as the breeze carried it past, she savored it, analyzed it—memorized it. There was no doubt. He was hers. The female's artificial floral odor could not begin to mask the heady scent of his pure blood. He would not get away, and even if he did, she would always be able to identify him now.

"I just needed some company. I've missed you." The saccharine sweet female touched him again, drawing closer as she stroked his arm.

Before she could stop it, a low growl rumbled deep within. In an instant, his head snapped toward her, glancing straight at the knoll, making her heart race. Had he heard her? Surely, he must have. Dragon hearing far surpassed human ears.

"You can't call me because you're in need of companionship. You've put us both at risk."

Stella poked her head up again. *Damn.* He had turned his back to her so that he stood between her and the human woman.

"You don't know what it's like to be all alone in the forest with nothing but your thoughts for company. If you're afraid she will find you, don't be. You're too fast and too cunning for that. You've proven that many times over."

The words twisted a knife in her chest. He had spoken to this woman about her. Had told her he'd been evading her.

"It's not *my* safety that concerns me. You're playing with fire."

"You think so? I'm not afraid. I know you'll protect me, even from *her*." The woman stepped away from him, spinning in a slow circle. "Do you hear me, dragon? He is mine, and I won't share, so just go away." She yelled the words into the night like a petulant child.

Every cell in Stella's body froze. How dare the woman lay claim to the man destined for her? Heat filled her chest, churning hotter and hotter with each passing second. Her skin prickled, and her jaw ached.

"That's enough," Brycen grabbed her and shoved her in front of him once more. "I will not tolerate your idiocy, Alexandra."

Stella waited, frozen in place, her breath caught in her throat. She listened for him to deny the woman's claim. Just once, she wanted to belong, to be someone's something, anything. She had known when she'd started seeking him out that there was a possibility he'd not want her, but to face it now was more than she could bear.

"Come to the cabin. We can spend the night together and get reacquainted. I've been so bored without you." The woman's pleas drove the knife deeper.

"For your safety, I will accompany you, but I won't stay."

"We'll see." The woman had the nerve to look back to the knoll before leading him from the clearing.

Stella sat on the trail with her head bent over her knees for hours after they had left. He hadn't returned. By the time the sky blazed with the pinkish-red hue of dawn, she had conceded defeat. His scent still lingered in her nose. He was *the one*. Somehow she had known all along he would be, but one whiff of his dragon's blood had confirmed it. He was hers and hers alone, yet he had chosen to be with the human. *Damn him, and damn her, too.*

She didn't bother to shower when she got home, she stripped and covered herself in her softest blanket, then forced herself to stay in bed, shoving the pain aside, until she drifted off to sleep.

The sun, so warm and welcoming on any other day made her want to scream when she woke with gritty eyes and the same lump in her throat she'd had before going to sleep. She tried to roll over and drift away again, but after another hour of tossing and turning, she gave up. With a drawn out groan, she tumbled out of bed, dreading what lay ahead. Although she had done it every night since she'd seen her mate in the forest, she still didn't relish putting herself out there. But she was no coward, and she was running out of time.

The gown she chose was a little too formal and way too revealing, but she needed the extra boost. She dusted her cheeks and put on some gloss. It didn't lift her sagging mood, but at least, he'd know what he was missing by choosing the human bitch over her.

Each night, she had sung her heart out, waiting—hoping—for the telltale tingles to let her know *he* was within hearing distance, but he hadn't shown, not yet. *He's probably too busy with that blond bimbo to have drinks with friends.* Even if she couldn't see deep into the pub's shadowed corners, her body would let her know if he came into the tavern. And now that she had his scent, he wouldn't escape, at least, not until she released him. Whether it was at the pub, in the forest, or in the middle of the Glen Farley streets, she would find him and free herself.

The smell of stale smoke and cheap whiskey filtered through the door before she reached it. Any other time, she would have turned away and saved her sensitive nose the trauma, but she couldn't stop, not now. He had made his choice, and now she was making hers, not that he had given her any other option. Sighing, she opened the heavy wooden door. She would endure yet another evening of endless propositions, leering glances from the men, and scathing looks from the women. It was almost laughable. If only they knew, she had no desire to have any of them, not a single smelly, disgusting one.

It was crowded, more so than the other nights. With the weekend approaching, the good—and not so good—people of Glen Farley were out in droves. The loud din of drunken voices had her wishing there was another way, but the way he kept running from her, she couldn't afford to wait. For once, she was glad the little town wasn't bigger with more nighttime entertainment options. It didn't matter that seeing him with that woman had torn her heart in two, or that nothing she'd ever find could replace what they could have had. She had to do what was right for her. She would release him and be done with it.

« CHAPTER 2 »

Why had he let Luke talk him into coming out? Brycen tipped his bottle back, letting the cold beer slide down his throat. It wasn't that he didn't like to go out and have fun, but he wasn't in the mood. In fact, his foul mood hadn't lifted since his meeting with Alexandra in the woods. The woman had all but goaded his mate into attacking. Had the she-dragon taken the bait, nothing he could have done would have stopped her from killing the idiot in her rage. He should have stepped aside and let her become she-dragon fodder for her idiocy alone. Of course, he wouldn't have, but after the stunt she'd pulled, she would have deserved it.

Had he known after all these years he would find his mate, no amount of money would have been enough to convince him to take this job. But the fact was he had, and until it was done, he had no choice but to keep Alexandra safe.

Brycen had yet to lay eyes on her, but she smelled like heaven, and *she* was looking for *him*. Once this job was over, he would be free to go to her. He would grovel and beg forgiveness, and he wouldn't stop until she accepted his claim. He just had to stay away from her for one more week, and then all bets were off.

Luke came back to the table with a tall brunette hanging on one arm, and an overly done blonde on the other. "Look what I found at the bar."

Brycen lifted one eyebrow. "I thought you were going for more beer." All he wanted to do was go back to the forest to finish his mission until his week was up, not deal with bimbos and drunkards.

"I was, but these two lovely ladies were standing there all alone with no place to sit, and since we have two empty seats, I thought I'd escort them back to the table before getting our drinks." He brought the brunette to his side of the table, claiming her for his own before settling the blonde next to him. "This is Julie, and that lovely lady is Christine. Keep them entertained while I get those beers." He winked at the girls before heading back to the bar.

Damn Luke for trying to set him up. He had nothing to say to these women, neither of them elicited a response anywhere near what just the scent of his mate did in him, but he wasn't a total bastard. He cleared his throat. Just then, a tingle starting at the base of his skull slid down his spine to land hot and heavy in his groin. The door swung open, allowing fresh air to carry the scent that tormented him day and night straight to him. *Shit.* He had to get out before she realized he was there.

The blonde next to him shimmied closer and put her hand on his upper thigh. He hadn't even realized she'd been talking, much less putting such a possessive move forward. He was going to kill Luke. "I'm sorry, ladies, I have to run." He shoved his stool back, letting her hand drop from his lap, fully intending to leave without saying another word, but his friend sat him down again.

"Hey, wait. She's here. That new singer everyone is raving about is coming on. Stay for a while. I heard her a few nights ago. I still can't get her sexy voice out of my head."

The brunette huffed, but stayed where she was, then smiled at Luke when he winked at her.

"Man, I can't. I have to go. You guys have fun, though." He made to stand again, but then a woman walked up the darkened stairs to the stage, and he froze. If he tried to leave now, she would spot him as he passed the stage on the way to the door. *Damn it. Fuck. Damn it.* Maybe there was a back door to this dive, and he could sneak out that way. When she stepped into the spotlight, he froze.

She cleared her throat, getting ready to speak into the mic when her head snapped up, and her gasp filled the room. She knew he was there. Her head bowed low, and for a second, it looked like she was going to turn and step off the stage again, but then she squared her shoulders and looked out into the crowd. Her big blue eyes didn't settle on him, but she was searching. His breath caught in his throat. That gorgeous creature with the long blond curls down to her waist was his mate.

Her ankle length gown covered her but concealed nothing. The lush curves of her hips and full breasts should have been for his eyes only. But every man in the place had already undressed her with their eyes, and he had to struggle not to growl at them all.

She scanned the room again, squinting against the spotlight illuminating her before clearing her throat again and grabbing the mic from the stand. "Good evening."

A shiver raced down his spine. The velvet heat in her voice had his cock twitching.

"My name is Stella. I'll only be singing one song for you tonight," she waited until the unhappy grumbles of the audience died down again, "and it will be my last performance here. I'd like to dedicate it to someone special. You know who you are." She took a shuddering breath, her sad smile betraying the chipper tone in her voice.

She cued the pianist, letting the soft melancholy notes carry through the room before lifting her head. No one uttered a sound. No glasses clinked. It was as though everyone in the entire room held their breaths.

"Come to me, I've been waiting for you." Her soft voice filled the room.

He couldn't tear his gaze away. What did she mean she wanted to dedicate it to someone special? His heart hammered. She wouldn't.

"I'll be whatever you need me to."

"Everything I'd leave behind for you."

"Come to me, I've been waiting for you." She closed her eyes as she sang, her free hand coming up to cover her heart.

Fuck. No, no, no. She couldn't do it, not now—not ever. He didn't even realize he was heading toward the stage until Luke's caught his arm.

"Where the hell are you going?" He tilted his head toward the women at the table.

The scales beneath Brycen's skin shifted, and Luke released his arm, taking a step back. "Hey, what gives? You can go if you want to, man, I just thought—"

"She's mine," Brycen cut in. The roughness in his voice had his friend's eyes widening.

Luke looked at the stage, then back at him with a huge grin. "*Damn*, dude. Her? You're one lucky bastard." His smile dropped as he heard the words she was singing. "Shit. She's releasing you. What the hell are you doing standing around here for?"

He clenched his jaw. "I can't claim her yet."

"Fuck that shit. The job isn't worth it. Get her." He shrugged when the women at the table grumbled and stood to leave. "Give me the coordinates and I'll take over with Miss Priss until you get back. Who's covering for you now, Jace?"

Sniffles sounded from women all around him. "Yeah." The song would be over soon, and if he didn't stop it before she said the words, he'd be screwed. He rattled off the directions to the cabin in the woods, knowing his friend would have no trouble finding it, and then turned back to the stage. Heading straight to the front, he pushed his way through the crowd.

The moment she opened her eyes, she saw him. Her voice quivered, and tears slid down her cheeks, but she didn't take her eyes off him.

"And I wish I could have meant more to you."

"Everything I am, I'd have given you."

"Release me, and I'll release you."

"Release me, I'm begging you."

His growl started deep in his chest, getting louder and louder until everyone around him took a step back. He didn't bother with the stairs, choosing instead to leap up in front of her.

"Release—"

"No." He didn't even feel sorry for interrupting the song. She'd said the words twice. One more time and that was it.

She shook her head, dropping the mic to her side. "P-please." Her eyes pleaded louder than her words.

He growled again, advancing on her like the predator he was. "No."

She opened her mouth to speak again, but by then, he had reached her. He silenced her with his lips in a hard, punishing kiss. *Release her, my ass. Not going to fucking happen.* Crushing her in his arms, he invaded her mouth, not caring who witnessed it. She melted against him and had it not been for the small distressed sound she made, he would have claimed her right there.

He pulled his head back, breathing her intoxicating scent into his lungs, tasting her on his tongue. Need, more intense than he had ever experienced shot through him, making him want to tear her sexy dress right off her body.

Pain, then fury, chased the dazed expression from her face. Shaking her head, she pulled out of his arms. "I'm nobody's mistress. Release me and you can go back to *her*, guilt free."

So desperate to keep her from breaking their bond, he had forgotten what she had seen, what she had undoubtedly assumed. He wasn't going to convince her of anything standing on stage with a crowd full of rowdy drunks watching and catcalling. Snapping his mouth shut, he picked her up, cradling her to his chest. When she struggled against him, he growled at her, meeting her glare with one of his own before throwing her over his shoulder. She wasn't going to get rid of him without at least hearing him out.

"Put me down this instant." She didn't raise her voice. She didn't need to. He would hear her if she whispered, even amongst all these people. The soft curve of her ass fit perfectly in his large palm, and he fought the urge to rub it as he held her snug against him.

When he ignored her and kept walking toward the door, she gave a frustrated growl that vibrated against his back. "Put. Me. Down," she snapped.

He couldn't help but smile, his mate had a temper. "Not until you hear me out."

"Put me down—please." The words were polite, but he'd bet his bottom dollar that she was already plotting her revenge.

"No."

She growled again, this time, more menacingly before she raised her hand and smacked him right on the ass. His chuckles joined the howling laughs from the drunkards nearest the door.

"I was going to wait until we'd done talking, but if you want to start with foreplay, I'm happy to oblige." He lifted his hand and smacked her ass as she'd done his, before rubbing it like he'd been wanting to do all along.

"Why, you arrogant, selfish, egotistical—"

"Don't forget sexy."

She stopped struggling. He was enjoying having this feisty she-dragon in his arms and wasn't about to set her down, no matter how much she wriggled. The door swung closed behind them, and he kept walking.

"Where are you taking me?" The small quiver in her voice had a fresh wave of heat rushing through him.

He rubbed a slow, gentle circle over the spot he'd spanked. She hadn't told him to stop, and although he couldn't feel the soft skin beneath the skirt, the last thing he wanted to do was stop touching her. So he kept on stroking. "Somewhere quiet so we can talk, and since I don't know where you live, my place it is."

"You can set me down. I can walk."

"Will you come willingly, then?" He made another rotation with his hand, slow and deliberate, knowing she was as affected by his nearness as he was by hers. He could smell her desire, and it fueled his own.

She sighed. "I'd rather you just say the words and be done with it so I can move on before..."

He stopped short and set her down in front of him, keeping her within reach in case she tried to bolt. "Before what?"

"Before it's too late." She bit the words out.

He leaned in close, his nose inches from her own. "Too late for what, precisely?"

"Too late for me to shift back." She glared at him.

Of all things, *that*, he hadn't expected. "Fuck. How close are you?"

Her gaze flicked to his shoulder. "Close."

He growled, drawing her gaze again. "How fucking close?"

"A few days, a week maybe, if I'm lucky," she choked out. "If you release me now, I may have enough time to find—"

"You'll find no one." His skin itched with the scales threatening to spring out from beneath it. Just the thought of any other male being near her made him want to roar, never mind having another's hands on her.

She swallowed hard. "You would deny me a full life?" She blinked fast, but not before he noticed the tears shimmering in her eyes.

"I deny you nothing."

"I told you, I am no one's mistress, and I meant it. I refuse to sit alone night after night waiting for someone who belongs to someone else." She clenched her jaw and tried to step away from him.

"I don't belong to anyone else, and neither will you." Many humans and even some dragons took on more than one lover, but he sure as hell wouldn't, and neither would she.

"I saw you in the forest. With her. Do you deny it? You never came back. You stayed there, all night— with *her*. I waited for you on that bloody trail for hours, and you never came back."

When she managed to squirm out of his grasp and took a step back, he took one forward. Her scent enveloped him, making his whole body ache with so much need he couldn't think straight. "I know what you heard, what you saw, and what you undoubtedly assumed. I'm telling you it isn't so."

"Fine, so you didn't spend the night with her. Whatever. You don't belong to her, so what?" She threw her hands up in the air. "Why, then, do you run from me? You knew I was searching, yet you hid and ran every time I got anywhere close. Am I so unbearable of a mate that you would rather be alone than with me?"

A heavy ball settled in the pit of his stomach at the sadness in her voice. He hated that she thought, even for a moment, that his reasons for not coming to her had anything to do with her. "I have obligations I cannot neglect."

"More important than a she-dragon trapped in her dragon form because her mate is too busy to claim her?" She shoved at his chest, the fiery spirit she'd shown earlier rearing up again. "You selfish bastard. Maybe I'm getting off lucky. I can find someone who will want to be with me, and only me."

He caught her hands and pulled her closer. "I thought I'd have more time. And you're right, I am selfish. Too selfish to allow you to find someone else, that's for damned sure. I didn't know you were close to the change. How could I?"

"Oh, I don't know, maybe you could have stopped running and spoken with me?" She spat the question at him.

"Damn, you are close, aren't you?"

She blew out a breath and nodded. "I ache all over. My skin feels like it's shrunk and no longer fits my body, and I can't keep my temperature steady."

"Come on. I can help."

Her pupils dilated, and she took a quick breath. "Where are we going?"

"My place."

« CHAPTER 3 »

Her killer stilettos were a perfect match for her blood red dress, but any more than a short walk would destroy her feet. "Is your place very far?"

He followed her gaze down to her feet. "I could always carry you. I don't mind," he said as he reached for her.

"You wouldn't dare." She took a step back, tugging at her hand, but his firm grip kept her where she was.

"Oh, I dare." With a quick flick of his wrist, he pulled her close before sweeping her off her feet, only, this time, to rest against his chest instead of over his shoulder.

"Umm... I'm Stella, by the way," she said as she closed her eyes and breathed him in.

His arms tightened around her, and he picked up his pace. "Brycen." The huskiness in his voice had her eyes popping open again.

"I can walk." She shifted to try to get down, but if she were honest, she liked being held close enough that she could hear his heart beating beneath her ear.

"If you walk, you'll take the shoes off when we get there. I want them on."

Had he shown any sign of strain, she might have argued, but he was practically jogging, and his breathing had yet to quicken. When he started a light stroke on the side of her breast with his thumb, it was all she could do to keep from twisting into the caress.

The dark stubble on his jaw begged to be touched, and why shouldn't she? He was hers, at least for now, and she could touch if she wanted to. The prickly hair tickled at her fingertips, a soft moan slipping past her lips at the thought of it tormenting other, more sensitive flesh popped into her mind.

"Shit, we're almost there. Hang on." He rounded one more corner, taking the first path on the right straight to a small bungalow. He didn't let her down until he reached the front door, and then, only long enough to fish his keys from his pocket to open it, and then slamming it closed with his foot.

He didn't break stride until he reached his bedroom. Lowering her legs, he slid her down his front, while keeping her close. As soon as her feet touched the floor, his free hand cupped her ass, pulling her tight against his hard length.

"Shouldn't we t-talk or something?" She couldn't drag her gaze from his lips. They were made for kissing, and she wanted another taste.

He ground himself against her. "We can talk if you want, but we both know that's not what you need. You're too close to the change." He bent his head to her neck, taking a sniff before licking from her collarbone to her ear. "I can smell the lust rolling off you."

She shuddered against him. "So what are you going to do about it?" There was no point in denying it. She did have needs, and right then, she would do anything to lessen the ache even just a little. She could get to know him later.

He didn't reply, choosing instead to nip at her jaw, groaning against her skin as she tilted her head, opening herself up to him.

The sting should have had her pulling away, but she moaned, pulling his hips into her again. Just rubbing up against his erection through the layers of their clothing had her trembling and close to orgasm. *God, yes.* The closer she had gotten to the change, the less she'd been able to take care of her needs. Try as she might, and in the beginning, she had tried, she just didn't have what her body needed to climax anymore.

"Don't." His voice snapped her out of the blissful fog.

"Don't what?"

"Don't come. Not until I say you can."

She groaned, her eyes rolling up as she shifted against him again. *So close, so, so close.* Later they could take their time, but right then, she needed an orgasm so bad it hurt.

With his hands on her hips, he stilled her movement.

"Please, Brycen, it's been so long." She closed her eyes tight, trying to regain control of her overheated body.

"How long?" His breath teased her lips.

"More than six months." Warmth crept up her neck. What the hell did it matter? She needed an orgasm, and he was the one who could give it to her.

"You haven't had a lover in over half a year?" He ground against her and pulled back again before she could find release.

She tried to push forward, but his strong grip prevented it. "No," she snapped. "I haven't had a lover ever. Period. I haven't had a fucking orgasm in six months. I can't get there on my own anymore."

He groaned and pulled away from her so fast she nearly stumbled. "You waited until you couldn't come anymore? Of all the asinine things I've ever heard." He shook his head, running his hands through his hair. "It's amazing you haven't gone off and killed someone." His eyes narrowed. "You haven't, have you?"

"No, of course not!" What kind of animal did he think she was? She straightened her dress as he paced away. Her pulse raced. "I'm sure if we just... if we just had sex—"

"Why did you wait?" His tone softened, and he paced toward her again. "You know as well as I do that it isn't about sex."

She swallowed once and then dropped her gaze to the floor. She didn't know, not really. "I didn't know what was happening. It's not like I could go to the local coffee shop and start asking the she-dragons enjoying their morning brew why I couldn't get myself off. And they don't have a how-to manual for dragons in heat at the local library."

He took her hand and waited for her to look him in the eyes. "Do you not have a sister, an aunt, or a friend you could have asked?"

He had to know that if he mated with her, he didn't get any of the perks of a clan backing her. No real financial benefit other than her meager savings. None of the affluence or power that should have been hers. All that disappeared on the day the hunters annihilated her clan. "What you see is what you get. Just me. I'm the last of my line," she said, refusing to break his gaze. So, you see, I can't risk losing the ability to shift. I need to be able to have children, and I can't do that if I'm stuck in dragon form."

Brycen closed his eyes and breathed deep. "Pureblood."

"It's been getting worse since I saw you on Tuesday. It's like she knows you're around, and she's pissed off that I haven't been with you yet."

He dropped her hand and walked to the other side of the bed. "Take everything off except for the shoes, and then come here."

When she hesitated for more than a second, he snapped his teeth, his growl rumbling between them. The sound sent a fresh wave of throbbing heat between her legs. Her breath hitched, but she did as asked, reaching behind her to slide the zipper down her back. The silent cascade of silk pooled at her feet followed moments later by her sheer lace bra.

"Stella?"

She pulled her bottom lip between her teeth, enjoying the strangled sound he made before taking a small step toward him. "Yes?"

"Where are your panties?"

She twisted her fingers together in front of her belly, the nervousness she'd all but forgotten rearing up again. "I didn't wear any. The dress... I didn't want panty lines."

"Put your hands down."

When she did, he looked at her from head to toe, then up again, taking his time. The only thing keeping her in place was the heated passion smoldering in his eyes.

"Good. Okay. Come here. You'll remove my clothes now," he said.

Oh God, he was going to make her take his clothes off. All she wanted to do was rip them to shreds. Having him this close and having to hold back was insane. Every part of her was set to break into a million pieces if he didn't do something soon.

A muscle ticked in Brycen's jaw, but he stayed where he was.

Putting a little extra sway to her hips, Stella rounded the bed, stopping only a hair's breadth away. She didn't stop to think for fear of losing her nerve. Fingers trembling, she undid the first button of his shirt, pulling the edges apart to reveal the top of his chest. She resisted the urge to rub her cheek against the exposed skin.

The next button came easier, as did the next until she had them all undone. Already, her breaths came in short gasps. His chest muscles rippled where her fingers touched as she pushed the shirt open and then slid it down his arms. She had known the hard wall of his chest would be glorious when he had carried her, but seeing it bare had her mouth watering. Not thinking, she leaned forward, and flicked the tip of her tongue over his puckered nipple, then pulled back at his sudden gasp.

"Were you given permission to do that?" he asked, his voice strained.

Her gaze flew up to meet his, but his eyes were closed, and he worked his jaw back and forth, grinding his teeth. Her heart thudded. They had only just begun, and already she had displeased him. "I'm sorry." She pulled her hands away.

"Tonight, I'm in charge. Do as I ask, nothing more." When he finally opened his eyes to look at her, his pupils were huge, almost covering the dark chocolate brown of his eyes. "Take my pants off now."

Gathering her courage, she reached for the snap of his jeans. His hot breath teased her bare shoulder, but she didn't dare look at him. Feeling around for the zipper, her fingers grazed the hard bulge straining against the denim. Heat rushed up her neck and cheeks when she heard him moan. She wasn't about to apologize again. If he wanted her to take his clothes off, he would have to deal with it.

Rather than bark more orders at her, he brought a hand up, guided hers to the tab, and helped her ease it down before lowering it to his side again.

She took a deep breath, his scent invading her, creating a pulsing beat at her core, or maybe it was just the nearness of the man. Whatever it was, she wanted more. With trembling fingers, she tugged at his jeans, sliding them down a couple of inches. When they wouldn't easily slip down past his hard length, she couldn't contain her grumbling sigh.

"Take your time." He brought his hand up to her shoulder, then up her neck to tilt her head to look at him. "I'm not going anywhere."

For a moment, Stella thought he might lean in and kiss her again. It would go a long way in bolstering her for what was to come, but he didn't. When his gaze drifted down to her lips, he snapped his mouth shut, dropped his hands to his sides again, and closed his eyes, waiting for her to continue.

Swallowing her frustration, she grabbed the thick denim along with his boxers, and yanked them down, tugging a little harder than necessary to get the job done. He may be sexy as sin and be the perfect match to her chemical makeup, but he didn't have to be an ass.

Brycen groaned, and she wondered if she had hurt him. An apology teetered on the tip of her tongue until she glanced up and found him grinning. "You may want to be easy with the goods, sweetling. It won't be of any use if it's damaged."

"If you'd help me, the *goods* would already be easing my discomfort," she huffed.

In one quick spin, he had her pinned against his dresser, the cold, hard wood digging into her bare ass. "What you want, and what you need are not the same, Stella. Lucky for you, I know what you need. The question is, are you woman enough to take it?" Brycen bent his head, whispering the last words into her ear before biting it—hard.

She jerked but didn't push him away. The throbbing pulse between her legs jumped with the slight pain and grew stronger, drawing a moan from her throat. The best she could describe the sensation inside her was—empty. Achingly empty. And he had what she needed.

She shoved his shoulders as hard as she could, sending him off balance. It wasn't much, but she gained the advantage. He was strong, but so was she, and it was high time he realized that. She pushed him again, shoving him until the back of his legs hit the mattress, and he fell on his back. "Oh, I'm woman enough." Stella climbed after him, not giving him time to move or even scoot further onto the bed. She took hold of his cock at its base, steadying the hard length as she straddled his hips, and then lowered herself onto him.

"Fuck, Stella." He gripped her hips, his fingers digging into her flesh.

"Yes, fuck Stella. That's what I want."

« CHAPTER 4 »

Brycen gave Stella a moment to enjoy taking control, giving the she-dragon a taste of what she was missing. His head was spinning with the need to claim her, to dominate, but both Stella and her dragon needed more. Stella had to relinquish control. The only way to appease the dragon was to allow *her* to take her mate, assuring that both she and Stella would be cared for in every way. Only once the dragon was satisfied that he would take care of all of their needs would she allow Stella to shift at will.

Stella had no clue what to expect from mating dragons. The beasts, both male, and female were stubborn, domineering, and protective by nature. Any other time, he would have accepted her submission, and enjoyed every second of it. The way Stella had instinctively bared her neck to him had made him hard as a rock, and it had taken all his strength to keep from biting down, and dominating her as *his* dragon demanded.

She deserved tenderness the first time they made love, but with her being so close to the shift, he couldn't give her that. It didn't mean he wouldn't ensure she enjoyed it.

Once she had taken a breath and was about to start moving over him, he rolled, taking her with him, flipping her onto her back in one smooth move. He thrust inside her, his cock pulsing in rhythm with her panting breaths.

When she slid her hands over his chest, he grabbed her wrists and trapped them against the mattress above her head. She writhed beneath him, her breasts only inches from his mouth, the hard nipples straining toward him. He wanted a taste so bad his cock twitched inside her, but he held back. If she wanted it, she had to take it. She'd waited too long to come to him—no, damn it—*he* had hidden from her, and now it was too late to coax the beast inside her with gentleness.

"Is that all you've got, Stella?" He didn't give her the opportunity to answer as he bit her shoulder, hard enough to sting and leave a mark. But not break the skin, and once again, she bared her neck to him. He groaned against her, licking the spot he had bitten, waiting for her next move.

She gasped and froze under him for half a beat, then bucked up, nearly throwing him off. Brycen chuckled, pinning her harder, and bringing his lips to an inch from hers. "You're feisty. My dragon likes that," he whispered. He thrust slow and deep, knowing she needed fast and furious, and she'd get it, but not yet. She wasn't ready. And if he were honest, he wasn't either. He wanted to savor as much of their first mating as he could. Crushing his lips to hers, he invaded her mouth, their tongues dueling as he rocked inside her.

Stella tore her lips from his, nipping at his bottom lip, "Brycen, please," she pleaded as she tried shifting beneath him, then growled when he held her in place.

Running his tongue along her jaw, and then down her neck, Brycen tempted fate again, scraping his teeth at the base. Damn but he wanted a taste. Her silken heat gripped him so fucking tight all he wanted to do was pound into her until they both flew apart. He was about to nip at her skin again when her nails raked across his back. "Let her come, Stella." He rocked inside her again, the head of his cock nudging her base with every slow thrust as he filled her.

Panting, she shook her head. "Can't. I won't be able to control her. She's waited too long."

"You don't have to. I will. She won't emerge tonight, not fully, but we'll calm her, and you'll feel better. Trust me." Unable to resist any longer, he lowered his mouth to her breast, circling the nipple with the tip of his tongue before sucking it between his lips. He sucked hard, swallowing his moan as her pussy clenched around him. She dug her fingers into his hair, tugging him closer. When he looked up, her eyes were closed, and her lush, red lips parted. It didn't take a lot of imagination to know how amazing sliding his cock past them and into her warm mouth would feel. He groaned at the thought, letting go of her nipple with a pop, stilling his hips.

"God, don't stop. Please," her voice hitched, "please," she repeated as she arched her back, bringing her breast close to his mouth again.

He hated that he had been the one to put that desperation in her voice—had caused her to suffer. "I'm not stopping, Stella, just taking a break. You feel so damned good, I'm not going to last if I don't, and I need to. Once we're fully mated, we can do fast and hard whenever you want, right now, your dragon needs something more."

Her eyes popped open, surprise shining in them. She didn't have a clue as to what she—and her dragon— needed. How long had she been alone? An unmated she-dragon should have had guardians, been pampered and protected by her clan, even if her family was gone.

What he wanted to do was shower her with all the pretty words she deserved, tell her she was beautiful, and that he would spend his life worshiping her. It wasn't just the chemical makeup drawing the two dragons together. Every inch of her appealed to him as a man, and if what little he knew of her personality held true, they'd be a perfect match. They *were* a perfect match. He'd tell her that he regretted staying away from her. That he wanted her, and only her, but that had to wait. He'd spend the rest of his life letting her know how precious she was, but right then, he had to deal with the rising dragon.

Bracing himself for a fresh onslaught of pleasure, he pulled back, then thrust deep inside her again, harder than before. His skin tingled as intense pulses of pleasure blasted through him. *Damn.* He had to find a way to push her into action. Otherwise, he didn't stand a chance.

***

Power, hot, and raw surged through Stella, driving her need higher. Each slow thrust Brycen made fanned the flames, heating the embers, but the last one, harder, faster, nearly had her tumbling over the edge of her orgasm. She wanted to let go, so much, but he hadn't told her to come yet. As much as she wanted—needed—release, she also wanted to please her new mate. She had gone half a year without an orgasm. A few more minutes wasn't going to kill her. Was it?

"You're thinking way too hard," Brycen said as he pulled all the way out, then slammed back into her. "Let the dragon out. It's the only way." More than the actual words, the new, deeper vibration in his voice had the beast inside her inching closer to the surface.

When he repeated the hard thrust, she rose up to meet him, taking him as much as he was taking her. Her sighs and whimpers grew louder and louder as he continued the onslaught. Pleasure filled every cell in her body. Everywhere he touched her, both inside and out, her flesh tingled with burning sensation, overwhelming her senses. Whether he liked it or not, she was losing the battle with her body. Her orgasm teetered only a couple of thrusts away, and as much as she wanted to, she wouldn't be able to stop it.

She closed her eyes tight as liquid heat flooded her. She couldn't catch her breath. Her nipples peaked, and with each of his thrusts, they rubbed against his chest, sending more pleasure whipping through her.

Without warning, he lifted his weight from her body and rolled off her, and onto his back. For a moment, she couldn't move, couldn't breathe. She whimpered at the sudden loss. When she opened her eyes and turned to look at him, his were closed, and he had a pained expression on his face. He took slow breaths through his nose, as he ground his teeth. He wouldn't even look at her.

"What happened? What did I do wrong?" She hardly recognized her voice with the hurt making its way around the lump in her throat.

"Jesus, Stella." He looked at her then, and she gasped. His eyes were molten gold, and his pupils elongated rather than round. "You didn't do a damned thing wrong. I want to bury myself in you and fuck you so hard that your teeth rattle, then I want to do it all over again because one time sure as hell won't be enough. By the time I'd be done with you, you wouldn't be able to walk, much less shift, but I can't do that."

She didn't understand. If it was what they both wanted, why the hell wasn't he doing it? Anger bubbled up inside her, almost, but not quite drowning out the hurt. Kneeling on the bed, she glared down at him. She wanted to lash out, but the words wouldn't come. Instead, she followed each hard line of his chest down to his waist with her hungry gaze, hesitating at his navel before moving lower. His long, hard cock stood at full attention, jerking when she finally stopped the visual exploration there.

Brycen moaned, and started to roll away from her. But before he could get to the edge of the bed, Stella was on him. In an instant, she was straddling his waist, with her hands on his shoulders. Her fingertips burned as she pressed into his flesh, and a growl rumbled free.

His eyes widened, and he emitted a low growl of his own. The vibrations rippled through his body, and into her where she straddled him, making her moan. His lips tipped up at the corners, drawing her attention. Licking her lips, she came down, stopping just shy of kissing him.

"Mine," she whispered in a low sultry voice before she claimed his lips. She tunneled her fingers through his hair, holding him in place as she drove her tongue into his mouth. The fiery heat rushing through her made her bolder, more aggressive in the taking, but she was beyond caring. He was her mate. *Hers*. And she would have him. All of him. Without breaking the kiss, she slid down his body, lifting off him only long enough to position herself, and coming down on his cock in one swift move. Nothing had ever felt better. A ripple of pleasure started at her core, spreading out to encompass her already throbbing body. She lifted her hips and took him again, barely aware that he had brought his hands to grip her there, helping her up, then down onto him hard again. But she didn't need his help, she was more than ready to take what was hers.

Stella sat up, her eyes locking with the liquid gold shining in his, as she brought his hands up to her breasts. The elongated pupils dilated further as he took their weight in his palms. Rolling her nipples between his fingers, he gave each a sharp tug. Stella moaned and threw her head back as she started moving in earnest over him. She leaned into his touch, anticipating the small measure of pain, which would morph into intense pleasure as he rolled her nipples again. When he kept the pressure on her nipples soft, she brought her gaze back to his. The moment she slid up his shaft again, heat sparked in his eyes, He gave her the sharp tug she needed and thrust into her in a hard upward stroke.

With her still straddling him, Brycen sat up. Before she could wrap her arms around his neck, he pulled her off him. She growled. A warning? An invitation? She wasn't sure, but he pulled her onto her hands and knees in front of him, his deep, masculine chuckle sending a shiver racing through her. With his arms on either side of her shoulders, he pinned her there with his weight. Rather than enter from behind as she expected, and desperately wanted, he just pressed into her. His growl came in soft, growing in intensity when she tried to wriggle against him to make him take her.

Deep inside, her dragon roared for release. Her entire body tensed beneath him. With more strength she even knew she possessed, she pushed up, ready to dislodge him, but he was ready for her. He growled again, closer to her ear this time, pressing harder into her back. His teeth scraped at her shoulder, longer, pointier than they had been, and she had to fight the urge to turn her head and snap at him. Not that she really could. He had her trapped between his arms, and back. She waited until his body melted into hers a little before bucking again, but he wouldn't budge.

All she heard was her own pounding heart and her quick pants while he kept her pinned beneath his powerful body. The throbbing she'd all but forgotten built again, deepening and pulsing in her core until she could hardly take it anymore. She whimpered, rubbing her ass up against his cock, silently begging for him to do something—anything—that would take away the aching need.

When he locked his teeth onto her right shoulder and growled again, she didn't dare budge, not even when he moved his arm to reach between them, guiding his cock to her entrance.

Without taking his teeth from her shoulder, he slammed into her in one long stroke. Stella cried out, in both pleasure, and the slightest bit of pain as he impaled her with his cock, but he didn't stop. She didn't want him to. His hard body still covered her as he thrust over and over, filling every bit of her with each stroke. When she tried to shift her weight to accommodate more of him, he bit a little harder. The dragon part of her wanted him to bite harder, to take her harder, so she wiggled against him as much as she could. His growl came in an instant, vibrating through him—through her.

Clenching her hands in the sheets, she moaned as the pleasure built higher and higher until she could hardly keep herself upright, but he didn't stop. Every beat of her heart sent a pulse straight to her core. She was close, so close. When he removed his teeth from her skin, she gave him a small growl of her own.

He brought his mouth to her ear, slipping his tongue along the shell. "You can come now," he whispered.

That was all it took. In an instant, her body quivered and shook. The pulses in her pussy deepened and strengthened as the muscles contracted and released around his shaft. She cried out as the pleasure exploded through her, sending her flying into nothingness where all that mattered, all that existed, was Brycen, and what he had done—was still doing—to her body. Even as her climax ebbed, he kept pounding into her. His grunts and moans fanned the flames higher again, so that when he clamped his teeth on her neck and gave one final thrust inside her, she shattered right along with him as he came inside her, milking every last drop from his body.

« CHAPTER 5 »

Stella woke from the blissful fog she'd slipped into with a leg draped over her hip, an arm tucked around her waist, and a hot chest pressed against her back. She couldn't remember the last time she'd had such a restful sleep. The constant aching need plaguing her over the past few months weren't gone, not entirely, but at least her body felt like her own again. With a contented sigh, she wiggled deeper into Brycen's warmth. If it weren't for the fact that she was starving, she'd never want to leave his bed again.

"Good morning, beautiful," he whispered into her ear, his voice still heavy with sleep.

Her heart beat a little faster. "Good morning." She started to turn to face him, but his arm tightened around her waist, preventing her movement.

"Stay where you are."

She was about to protest when he pressed his lips to her neck, kissing the tender skin where he'd bitten her. He slid his hand up her belly to her breast, then moaned as she pressed closer.

He kneaded her breast, working his way to the tip. "I love how you respond to me. Your nipple is already hard and waiting. Makes me wonder what other parts of you are anxious for my attention."

With nothing more than a small kiss and his warm hand, her body pulsed to life. "All of me." She wasn't ashamed to admit her need, even if she was, denying it would be useless. With his dragon's sensitive nose, he'd be able to smell her desire, just like she could his. It was intoxicating knowing that her mate wanted her just as much as she wanted him.

"Let's see then, shall we?" The second he lifted the leg still pinning her down, she missed its weight. She wanted to burrow closer to him, not put space between them. Stella held her breath when he released her breast and slid his hand down her belly. His cock jerked against her ass. She moaned and spread her thighs open a little wider, needing whatever it was he was giving.

"That's right. I want you to open yourself up for me."

Instead of going straight for her pussy, he slid his palm down her thigh, then lifted her leg to drape it over his bent knee, exposing her completely. "Look how beautiful you are. How wet you are. And I haven't even touched you yet." He smoothed his fingertips down her inner thigh, pausing just inches from where she needed his touch most.

"Brycen..."

"Look. I want you to see it. See how much you want me. Watch me love your body."

Until then, she hadn't noticed the large mirror in front of her, or that she was on full display. When she met his gaze in the reflection, she saw the pure lust, the possessiveness in the depths of his eyes, and her heart pounded. She was his. He was hers.

He pressed his lips to her neck, kissing the deep red spot he had left with his bite, then scraped his teeth against it. Moving his fingers in small circles on her inner thigh, he brought her attention to that spot. Heat curled inside her, then settled on her clit, making it throb. When his fingers finally slid between her parted folds, Stella moaned, closed her eyes, and thrust her hips forward, wanting more.

Brycen's fingers stopped moving. "Keep your eyes open. Watch what I'm doing. I want to see them when you come for me."

When she did as he asked, he stroked her clit again, circling over and around it until she could hardly lay still. She concentrated on keeping her eyes open, on watching his fingers, shiny with her arousal, teasing her.

"More than six months without an orgasm. I bet you're ready for another one, aren't you?"

She opened her mouth to respond, but that's when he chose to slip not one, but two fingers inside her, and her mind went blank. Her pussy clenched around him, and she moaned at the invasion. Each time his fingers disappeared into her body she held her breath until they skimmed across the tender spot inside her that made her whole body tremble. She wanted more—needed more. Wanting to feel the hard length of his cock sliding in her palm, she reached behind her, but he stopped her with a growl.

"This is for you, Stella. Last night, we took care of the dragon. Now, I want to take care of my woman. Let me do that." Even as he caught her gaze in the mirror, his fingers continued to plunge inside her. He moved faster, rubbing against that spot over and over. Brycen brought his lips to her neck again, kissing her mark, nipping at the skin, then licking it. The sensation had her gasping for air and the muscles in her thighs trembling. "Are you ready to come for me, little dragon?" he whispered into her ear just before he used his thumb to stroke across her clit.

A wave of intense pleasure rushed through her, and she cried out. She met his gaze in the mirror, unwilling to look away as he sent her flying higher and higher. He thrust faster and harder, swiping his thumb across her clit. She wanted to hold out, to make it last, but when he put his lips to her neck again, she was lost. One final nip on her skin and she shattered around his fingers. It took everything in her to keep her eyes open. Brycen gentled his thrusts as she came down from her climax. Only once her breathing slowed, and the spasms rocking her core subsided did he pull his fingers from her body. She watched as he brought them up to his lips and tasted her.

***

Never in his life had Brycen seen anything hotter than Stella having an orgasm. When she came around his fingers, it had taken all his strength not to turn her over and fuck her fast and hard. Not that he thought she would have minded, in fact, he would have made sure she loved every second of it, but he couldn't focus on his needs. Stella, and making sure she gained the ability to shift, had to be his one and only priority. Once the she-dragon was satisfied, he could take all the time in the world to explore his mate and fuck her every way until Sunday. And he would. Jace and the others would have to do without him for however long it took, and from the looks of it, it might take a while.

The sexy sounds she made before and after coming had his cock so hard that he could feel his heart beat in his shaft. Torturing himself a little more, he pressed his hips forward, then moaned as his cock slid against the soft skin of her ass.

Stella stretched and smiled at him in the mirror. "It's time to take care of you now." Before he could stop her, she disentangled their legs and turned so that they were face to face.

He tried to ignore the softness of her skin, and the hard points of her nipples against his chest, and most of all, how close he was to being able to slide into her tight pussy. All it would take would be a flex of his hips, and he would be inside her. When her small hand closed around him, he couldn't help thrusting into it.

She had just tilted her face up to kiss him when her stomach gave a loud, hungry growl. She blinked up at him, and then the cutest pink blush crept up, staining her cheeks. He tried not to laugh. He really did, but the mortified look on her face had him chuckling as much as hearing her stomach making its demands. The more he tried to stifle it, the harder his chest shook. "I appreciate you wanting to reciprocate, but I think we better get you fed."

"It's okay. I'm not that hungry," her denial only made him laugh harder.

"That may be true, but I'm starving," he insisted. He kissed the tip of her nose, then pulled her hand from where she had it wrapped around his cock. "Don't worry. As soon as I have you fed, I plan to take full advantage of your willingness to explore my body. I'll tell you what? Go ahead and have a shower. By the time you're done, breakfast will be ready and waiting." She opened her mouth, presumably to protest, so he silenced her with a kiss that left him throbbing again. When he finally pulled his lips from hers, he stood and stepped away. If he were any closer, he'd just kiss her again, and who knew how long it would be until he provided her with food. He wanted to take care of her, yes, but he also had to prove to the she-dragon that he was a suitable mate. One that could provide for her and keep her safe if she was unable to do so herself.

Stella didn't look away as he grabbed a pair of boxers and slipped into them. Her pouty lips almost had him coming back to kiss her again, but then she darted her tongue out to lick them, and he groaned.

There was no way he'd settle for just a kiss if he went back to her. "You're killing me."

"Still want breakfast?" she asked as she got on all fours and came toward him.

"Hell no, but I'm getting you breakfast if it kills me. Maybe I have some cold cereal in the cupboard somewhere that you could eat *while* you shower."

At that, Stella laughed, the sound rich, and sensual, slid over him, making him question the need for sustenance even more. Dragons had voracious appetites that mostly revolved around protein. It took a lot of energy to create fire and to haul a huge ass dragon across the sky, and whatever stale, sugar coated, cardboard bits that passed as cereal these days he might find in the pantry just wouldn't cut it, and they both knew it.

He closed his eyes and took a deep breath, readjusting his boxers. When he opened them again, he found her sitting on the edge of the bed with her hair cascading over her shoulders like spun gold.

"Right, breakfast." He forced himself to step back. If he went anywhere near her, they wouldn't leave the bedroom at all. The way she was looking as though she wanted to devour him whole, her shower wouldn't take long, and if he wanted to feed her, he'd

better have it ready by the time she came into the
kitchen.

« CHAPTER 6 »

The moment Brycen left the bedroom Stella threw herself back on the bed and smiled up at the ceiling. Her whole body tingled with awareness. The dragon inside her was calm, for sure, but not exactly satiated. It wanted more. More skin on skin, more Brycen. More everything.

After witnessing the scene in the forest between Brycen and that woman, even though it would have crushed her, Stella had resigned herself to finding someone else. Any other man, dragon or otherwise, would have been a poor substitute. The fact that Brycen, not only was willing but seemed just as eager as she was to bind them together, made her want to laugh and throw herself on him. And she would, the moment she was done with her shower. Her stomach growled again, but it would have to wait. She had a mate to spend time with, and the sooner she was done, the sooner she could go find him.

The bathroom, like his bedroom, was neat and tidy but had little personality. Plain white walls, and surfaces devoid of dust. There were no pictures or ornamentation anywhere as far as she could tell. It just was. The shower itself was huge. She spread her arms wide, gauging the size. They definitely would both fit and have plenty of room to move around.

A flash of color on her arm drew her attention. Deep, dark purple, the same shade she had seen on her mother, skimmed just beneath her skin. Gasping, she brought her arm up for closer inspection. Scales. She wasn't ready for scales. She and Brycen weren't fully mated. Heart racing, she rushed through her shower. She took a moment to towel dry her hair, then finger comb it, before rushing back into the bedroom and throwing on a T-shirt she found in his top drawer.

The smell of cooked meat mingled with the scent of her mate reached her the moment she opened the bedroom door. She followed it, ignoring the grumbling still going on in her stomach until she found him sitting at a small round table with a single plate set directly in front of him.

Forgetting her scales, she glanced at the counter, only to find it bare. He had fixed breakfast for himself, but not for her. Hmmph.

When he looked up, the heat in his gaze was almost enough to make her forget his negligence—almost.

"Come here, beautiful." He pushed his chair back from the table and spread his knees, giving her a spot to sit on his lap.

"I wouldn't want to interrupt your breakfast," she bit out. She meant to stay where she was, but when he held his hand out she came closer. The moment his fingers wrapped around hers, he pulled her the rest of the way, settling her on his lap.

"Interrupt *my* breakfast?" He leaned in and pressed a chaste kiss on her lips. "Sweetheart, this isn't my breakfast. It's yours. Well, technically, I suppose it's ours, but if you want it all, I'll make more."

That was when she noticed the oversized plate and the massive steak taking up most of the space on top of it, with cheese and eggs filling the rest. A bowl of fruit, cut into bite-sized pieces, sat next to the plate, along with two tall glasses of orange juice.

"Oh." Heat raced up her neck and into her cheeks.

"You thought I'd make myself something to eat and ignore your needs?" he asked. "Of course you did. The way I kept running from you, it's no wonder you don't trust that I'll take care of you."

"I'm sorry. I just assumed—"

"Don't. I'm the one who needs to apologize. I'm sorry I didn't come to you the moment I knew you were near. I'm sorry I wasn't there to help you through the changes you've been going through. But I'm here now. And I won't let you down again. You have my word on that."

A lump grew in Stella's throat, and she could only nod. This man was hers. This gorgeous, strong, wonderful man, was her mate, and she wasn't going to spend a single moment dwelling on what happened in the past. Only the present and future mattered.

"Now, let's get you fed. The way you look in that t-shirt makes me want to rip it off you and take you right here on the table."

Brycen pulled her in tight against his chest and pressed his lips to her neck. She wiggled against the hard bulge under her, smiling when he moaned against her skin.

"You know, two can play that game." He reached around her, cutting into the steak, spearing into a piece with a fork, then bringing it up to her lips. "Open."

She did as he asked. Perfectly cooked, medium rare, with just the right amount of seasoning, the steak practically melted in her mouth. Closing her eyes, Stella moaned as she chewed.

The soft clink of utensils scraping against porcelain had her opening her eyes again. "So delicious, thank you."

"You're welcome." His voice was a little deeper, huskier than it had been. He brought another piece of meat to her lips, then once she'd taken it, took one for himself before setting the fork and knife down.

He brought his hands up, cupping her breasts, the warmth radiating from his palms making her nipples tighten. He rolled them through the thin material, tugging at them, sending jolts of pleasure racing through her. Too soon, he reached for the fork again, repeating the process of feeding them both. When he finished, rather than come back to her breasts, he slid his hands down to her knees, lifting them to drape them over his own, spreading her open. Wearing nothing more than his T-shirt, her naked flesh tingled in the cool air. On the way back up, he eased up her thighs, hooking the cotton with his thumbs, so it bunched at her waist.

With a feather light touch, he stroked lazy circles on her inner thighs, so close, yet nowhere near close enough. The slow, sexy torture continued while he fed her. After each bite, he teased a different area, brushing closer and closer to the intimate caress she craved, but never quite reaching it.

"That's not fair. You still have your boxers on." Her body was on fire, the throbbing pulse between her legs making her ache with need.

"True, but you're the one who was misbehaving and wiggling that gorgeous ass of yours all over my cock."

"So what happens if I do it again?" she asked, not bothering to wait for his answer before she ground herself against him. Now that her belly was full, nothing was stopping her from taking what she wanted most. Him.

His fingers tightened on her thighs, and he moaned. "Then you go back to bed without finishing your breakfast," he said just before he nipped at the skin of her shoulder.

"I can live with that." She tried to wiggle again, but he held her in place.

"We're almost done. Let me take care of you." Shoving the plate aside, he plucked a piece of melon from the bowl he'd prepared. When he brought it to her mouth, he spread the juice on her lips before letting her take it. He watched as she chewed, his lips parting when she darted her tongue to the corner of her mouth, and then with a groan, he kissed her. His tongue swiped over her lips before delving inside.

He finally pulled back, and went for another piece of fruit, but she reached out, stopping him. "I swear I'm full. Just take me back to bed. The only thing I want right now is you."

"Is that so?" Without waiting for her to answer, he helped her to her feet before turning her to face him. "Maybe I don't want to wait until we get to the bedroom. You look good enough to eat with my T-shirt on."

She grinned up at him, wrapping her arms around his neck when he grabbed her butt and pulled her tight against him. "So what are you waiting for?"

He eyed the table behind her and sighed. "That will have to wait. As much as I want you spread eagle on the table for me to feast on, it would be uncomfortable for you to stay there that long. I'd need more than a few minutes to satisfy that hunger."

He lifted her, so she stood on tiptoes, sliding his hands down her thighs until she wrapped her legs around his waist. The moment he stepped toward the bedroom, she nuzzled his neck, licking and nibbling at his skin. His sharp indrawn breath and tightening grip on her ass made her bolder. Never had she wanted anything more than she wanted her mate at that moment. "I'm the one who's going to be feasting," she whispered in his ear before catching the lobe between her teeth and giving a sharp little tug. "I'm going to lick every inch of you before I take your cock into my mouth…"

Brycen moaned as he crossed the threshold taking them back into his room. Before she knew what he was doing, she was on her back with his weight pressing her into the soft mattress. With her legs still locked around his waist, she pulled him closer, cursing when she realized he still wore his boxers.

"Get rid of them," she ordered even as she tried tugging them down.

When the phone on his nightstand rang, Brycen stiffened but didn't move except to lower his mouth to hers. He teased her with light, sensual strokes, making her want to scream in frustration and melt at the same time.

After what felt like forever, the ringing stopped, and he kissed along her jaw, then down her neck to her shoulder before tracing her collarbone with his tongue.

When his phone rang, this time with a more annoying, shrill sounding tone, she wanted to grab it and throw it against the wall. Brycen tensed, and then in an instant, he was pulling away from her.

"Damn it. I'm sorry. It's work. I have to take this." If the frustration in his voice was anything to go by, he wasn't any happier at the interruption than she was.

"Of course, take the call." She hadn't even thought about how their mating would affect his life. She had had little choice in the timing of things, but the least she could do was be understanding when he had to work. Now that she knew they would be mated, the panicky feeling that had made her crazy over the past weeks subsided. Things would be okay.

Wanting to give him a bit of privacy to take his call, she wiggled away, intent on getting off the bed, but his soft growl stopped her.

"Stay right where you are, this won't take long," he said.

Meeting his gaze, she nodded and lay down again while he sat on the edge of the bed with his back turned to her and grabbed the phone.

"This had better be fucking important," he bit out as he answered the call.

He sat stock still, listening to the person at the other end. The muscles in his back tensed more and more as he listened.

"Shit. Listen, Jace, I can't deal with this. I'm with my mate—" He paused to listen to the person on the phone, "Yes, *my mate*, damn it. I can't leave her right now. Get Luke on this. He can track just as well as I can, maybe even better."

"Shit." Brycen groaned, and his shoulders slumped a little. "Right. Meet me at the cottage. We'll start from there."

His knuckles were white with the grip he had on the phone when he returned it almost too gently onto the table. He didn't face her right away, instead, taking a deep breath, then another.

"It's okay." Stella wasn't sure what was going on, but she'd gotten the gist of the one-sided conversation. She could wait for him to get back. "Will you be gone long?"

"A few hours at most, it shouldn't take much more than that." He looked at her then, his jaw set. "I'm not going to start our relationship with lies, not even ones of omission. I have to look for Alexandra, the woman you saw with me in the woods. She's gone missing."

What the hell? In an instant, her insides heated and the muscles in her abdomen clenched as jealousy burned hot and bright in the pit of her stomach. Only the fact that he didn't look any more pleased about it than she did, calmed the fury.

The hurt from the past weeks bubbled up to the surface again, but she shoved it down. He wasn't running from her anymore. It was his job, nothing more. "It's okay."

"Stella..." When he turned to face her again, his eyes pleaded for understanding. "I would give anything to stay here with you, but I wasn't given a choice. As soon as we find her, I'll have one of the others take over the assignment, and I'll come home. To you."

She nodded, giving him what she hoped was a confident smile. "I believe you." And she did. Even though he had initially hidden from her, he hadn't given her any doubts about his intentions from the moment they had met the night before. "Go to work. I'll be waiting when you get back."

Reaching down, he took her face between his hands and took her lips in a sweet kiss that left her yearning for more. "Make yourself comfortable and rest while I'm gone. When I get back, I intend to complete our mating, and you'll need all the extra energy you can get."

« CHAPTER 7 »

Brycen stomped through the forest, not caring who heard. Of all the times for Alexandra to go running off without protection, this was the worst. Stella needed him, and where was he? Chasing after Alexandra of all people. If she wanted to play games, she'd be in for a disappointment. He wasn't in the mood. Every cell in his body screamed in protest with every step he took further away from Stella. The sooner he could find the spoiled brat and deliver her to Jace, the better.

His skin prickled as his scales poked below the surface, responding to the anger flowing through him. Nothing should come between him and his mate, not work, and certainly not the self-absorbed woman he was tasked to protect.

Before going to the cabin, he headed to the clearing where Alexandra had asked him to meet her before, hoping she'd gone there to wait for him. Too late, he realized two things, one, the animals were quiet—too quiet. And two, the air reeked of human sweat and fear, and a whole lot of excitement.

He should never have let his guard down. Thoughts of Stella and the need to get back to her had taken his focus from his surroundings—huge mistake.

There hadn't been any hunting activity in the woods for well over a year, at least, none that didn't involve game and wildlife. Since they had circumvented a dragon raid almost a year ago, things had been quiet in the area. Up until a few weeks ago, he would have welcomed the distraction of tracking and eliminating a group of dragon hunters. But with Stella waiting for him at home, engaging the enemy was the last thing he wanted to do.

He sniffed the air again, this time using more of his dragon senses. He caught a faint familiar scent coming downwind and had to keep from growling. If they didn't know where he was, he sure as hell wasn't going to lead them to him by being more careless than he already had been. The sound of a snapping twig around the bend of the dirt path he'd been on had him ducking behind a thick patch of bushes.

"You said he'd be here." A deep male voice with a heavy southern accent reached Brycen long before he saw the man come around the bend with

Alexandra at his side. Of average height, the man stood maybe six inches taller than Alexandra, but there was no mistaking his solid build. He would pack a mean punch if he managed to land it.

She smiled up at the man, reached and squeezed his bicep, and then giggled as she leaned closer. "He will be. And he'll bring his friends. You'll have beautiful trophies to put on your walls. You just have to be patient, Trevor. And if you're lucky, Brycen will bring his dragon bitch into the forest, and you can hunt her as well. I hear he's mated her already. It's rare to bag a female dragon these days. There are so few of them left."

Brycen's vision changed from normal colors to red as the dragon inside him surged forward. No one would threaten his mate—no one. Everything in him wanted to attack the couple, but something held him back. Hunts of these types didn't come cheap and weren't a solitary endeavor. Going after dragons alone was tantamount to suicide. There had to be more hunters nearby.

The man stopped in his tracks and looked at Alexandra as though she'd just given him a winning lottery ticket. "Darlin' if you can make that happen, I'll double what we're paying you," he said, proving that there were more of the bastards out there somewhere.

Alexandra looked up at him, batting her eyelashes. "I can't guarantee it, those dragons tend to be a little over protective, and very overbearing when it comes to their mates, but I'll tell you what? If she comes along, and you get a shot at her, maybe you can pay me for the bonus in other ways." She stepped closer to the man, brushing her breasts against his arm.

"I'll pay you *that* bonus whether the dragon bitch shows up or not, Lexie. What's a beautiful girl like you doing organizing a dragon hunt, anyway?" Trevor wrapped his arm around her waist, pulling her closer, all the while, leering at her overflowing cleavage. The gold band on his left ring finger sparkled in the sunlight.

"Easy money. I get paid well for what I do, and usually, when the carnage happens, I'm long gone, so they're none the wiser. The only reason I'm still here this time, is because they insisted on keeping me in a damned cabin with no way to get back to town without one of them getting me there. I'm just lucky I was able to get back here to meet up with you guys before anything happened."

"Trev, keep your dick in your pants. Something is brewing. I can feel it in my bones. Time to bag some dragons." Another man's voice came down the trail. For people who thought themselves dragon slayers, they didn't try to be quiet.

Trevor grinned down at Alexandra and grabbed her breast, squeezing it in his hand even as the other man came into view. "What's going on Bill, I was just getting better acquainted with Lexie."

"There's some movement on the other side of the clearing. It's gotta be the dragons."

Brycen sniffed the air, and sure enough, he caught a whiff of both Luke and Austin. If they were there, Jace wasn't far behind. He should have gone to the cabin first like he'd told Jace on the phone, but he'd gambled on finding Alexandra here and dropping her off so he could get back home. If they were there, chances were that at least they had been paying attention and had noticed the hunters in the area.

His skin prickled again, and it took all he had to keep from moving and giving away his position. There were more men around, but where? Surely, they weren't stupid enough to stand in the clearing and wait for dragons to show up. No, they had to be in the forest around him. All he had to do was wait for them to show themselves.

"Let's get into position, boys," the one named Trevor announced.

At least Brycen wouldn't have to worry about warning his friends. Even if they didn't already know about the hunters, the racket the humans were making would be heard for miles around.

Out of the corner of his eye, the slightest movement caught his attention. A man, no more than twenty feet to his left shifted, giving his position away. Brycen shrank down lower. Sheer luck was all that had kept the man from looking toward the brush and seeing Brycen hunkered there. His face painted in camo, matched his outfit. This one was serious about the hunt.

Brycen waited until the man moved forward and joined his friends on the trail before breathing again. The small group had just disappeared around the bend when the hiss of an arrow slicing through the air right next to his head had him ducking. *Fuck.* The bastard hadn't made a sound. He turned his head, searching for the hunter, but nothing moved. *Damn it.*

Staying where he was wasn't an option. The hunter already had his location. Shifting would give the bastard a bigger target, but if he could get into the air, he had a chance of getting out of range. He needed a few seconds to shift, and another few to get into the air. If he could get the man to shoot without actually hitting him, he'd have a shot before the hunter could draw again.

Grabbing a pebble at his feet, Brycen tossed it a few feet away, hoping the sound would divert the hunter's attention, if not draw his fire. The moment the stone landed, the whine of another arrow cutting through the air sounded. Focusing his thoughts and energy, Brycen shifted and took a deep breath. It dug into a tree less than a foot from where Brycen now stood in dragon form. With a mighty flap of his wings, he lifted from the ground. With the other hunters so close, he didn't dare roar or breathe fire, though he'd love more than anything to do just that. *Kill the filthy humans who wish to harm our mate.* The dragon's voice roared in his mind.

Not yet. Never had it been so hard to keep the dragon from raging, but Brycen held onto his iron-clad control. *First we get to safety. Then we attack with our clan. We can't take chances. We have to get back to Stella.*

He pushed himself hard, getting to the top of the tree line before fire sliced through his left side. His furious roar shook the nearby trees as he climbed higher into the air. In an instant, more arrows flew, but none of them reached him. Not that it mattered, he'd been hit. It was only a matter of time before he came down again.

Brycen fought the lethargy, keeping his wings flapping hard and himself just out of range for as long as he could until the weight of his body started dragging lower. The land beneath him blurred, and he tried to come down for a soft landing, but his muscles wouldn't cooperate. Bones crunched, and the ground shook as he crashed through trees and onto the forest floor. Hundreds of birds took flight, squawking at his unexpected landing, but Brycen didn't hear any of them as all went black.

« CHAPTER 8 »

Stella stretched and opened her eyes. Her whole body ached, but not the same sweet ache she'd had the previous day after she'd made love with Brycen. No, this was different—unpleasant. Her skin itched, burned even, and her jaw popped in the wrong spot when she tried to yawn. The orange glow of the rising sun told her what she already knew. He hadn't come back.

When Brycen had left the day before, he'd told her to make herself at home, and she had. Preparing a nice dinner for them both had occupied her for a while. But when it had become apparent he wasn't going to be home for the meal, she finally gave in and ate her portion, then stuck his in the fridge to eat later.

There was no point in staying in bed. Stella was wide-awake and worse, the dragon inside her was restless. Heat radiated from her, making her skin clammy. Heading into the bathroom, she couldn't help notice that her legs didn't move as fluidly as they should. It was as though the joints didn't quite fit together right. Heart pounding, she turned the faucet to cool then stepped into the shower. All she had to do was keep the dragon happy until Brycen returned. Then they could take care of this once and for all.

"Come on, mate. I need you," she whispered as the cold water sluiced down her body. She took her time, washing and rinsing her hair, oddly pleased when she smelled more like him after using Brycen's shampoo. Inside, the dragon settled a little as though that small connection with him pleased her as well.

"When will he be back?" Stella gasped and froze when the soft rumbling voice sifted into her mind. *"We need him now."*

Stella waited for a moment, reveling in her dragon's voice. She'd wished to hear it so many times, but the beast had remained quiet all those years. *"I don't know. I want him back, too,"* she finally answered.

The flash of purple under her skin had her heart racing. *"He'll be back. He'll take care of us. Please, don't do this,"* Stella begged. All she needed was a bit more time. Everything she had ever wanted, a partner, a family, it was all within her grasp. She just had to hang on a little while longer.

She waited for a response, but nothing came. When even the shower's spray couldn't keep her comfortable, she toweled herself off and headed back to the bedroom. If the dragon liked Brycen's smell, she'd surround herself with it. Riffling through his drawers, she found a pair of sweatpants with a drawstring. She'd have to roll them up so she could walk, but it would work. She eyed the soft sweaters in another drawer but dismissed them just as fast. She was already burning up, what she needed was another T-shirt. She found one and slipped it over her head. Too uncomfortable in her skin, Stella didn't bother with her underwear.

She spent the next hour and a half pacing all over the house from one room to the other. She paused here and there to touch his things. There wasn't a lot there. But when she found something that was a little more personal, like the half read book he had left on the coffee table, she slid her fingers over it. Or clutched his pillow to her chest and took his scent into her lungs.

Time was irrelevant, but she couldn't help glaring at each clock as she walked past. *Where the hell is he?* Her discomfort grew with each passing minute until she couldn't stand the pacing anymore. Something wasn't right. If he could be there with her, he would. But that didn't stop her irritation from climbing or lessen her need for movement. The energy pulsing in her grew hotter, desperate, and she had no idea what to do to, or how to release it.

She had to get out of there. Stella had never been claustrophobic, but she had to get outside, somewhere with a big, open space. Every room in the house was too small.

She didn't bother changing back into her clothes. She could hardly stand her stilettos when she wasn't in pain, much less now, and just the thought of putting her dress back on and taking his scent off her skin had her growling. She'd just go with what she had on.

She found a notepad and scribbled her address on it as best she could with her shaking hands, then headed out the door.

By the time she reached her house, the cuts and scrapes at the bottoms of her feet left a trail of blood for anyone to follow, but she didn't care. The pain was nothing compared to the fiery inferno inside her chest. Breathing was more than difficult. It was near impossible. She panted as she walked but kept putting one foot in front of the other.

She stopped long enough to pull a well-worn pair of sneakers onto her bare feet before heading out again. She didn't know where she was going, only that she had to keep moving. Only when it became apparent that she was making her way to the mountain, did she allow her fear to take root. *"Please, hold off for a few more hours. He'll come for me—for us—I know he will,"* she begged the dragon. *"He will not let us down. He promised."*

Her pleading went unanswered. She fought the compulsion to keep moving forward, but her body wouldn't listen, the dragon's will overshadowing her own. Tears streamed down her cheeks. The dragon was searching for a den. She wouldn't want to live with humans or be a part of *their* world any longer. She would do her best to keep Stella safe and well fed, but in the end, the loneliness of a solitary existence would do them both in.

Stella ignored the sun climbing overhead. She'd been walking for hours, but she didn't care. The higher into the mountain she climbed, the fewer landmarks she recognized. Even if she managed to stave off the shift this time around, there was no way she'd be able to find her way back to Glen Farley before the next wave hit.

By the time she finally stopped moving, the sun had crossed the sky and every muscle in her body ached. She took a deep breath and looked around. A wide yawning hole in the rock face about twenty feet above her head drew her attention. So, that was to be where she lived from now on. Without a mate to protect her, the cave made sense. As a dragon, it would be easy to get to, yet hard for the enemy to penetrate. When the dragon pushed her forward again, she didn't even bother trying to stop it. If she slipped and fell, at least she wouldn't have to live in the damned cave for the rest of her life.

When she finally made it up to the entrance, Stella didn't dare stop. If she did, even for a second, she wouldn't make it into the cave and relative protection from the elements, and as exhausted as she was, who knew how long she'd be there? With her hands scraped raw, she felt her way into the dark cavern, hoping that no animal had made a home there before her.

She had only taken a few steps, and several breaths of the dank, musty air when her eyes adjusted to the darkness. The reddish tinge in her sight made her more aware of the dragon's presence than ever.

As far as caves went, she had to admit, it wasn't bad. There were plenty of flat surfaces for her to lie on, and it was big enough that even shifted, she would be able to move around. She didn't bother looking in all the little nooks and dips in the walls. Even if there were other creatures in residence, she didn't have the energy to fight them off or chase them away.

She found an area where the rock floor was smooth and somewhat hidden from the entrance before collapsing. Sighing, she closed her eyes. There was no point in crying over what could have been, but still the tears fell. She pulled Brycen's T-shirt to her nose and breathed in his scent, willing him to appear, yet knowing he wouldn't.

« CHAPTER 9 »

Fire raced through him as Brycen fought to breathe through the pain. The impact had been hard. He'd broken a few bones, but those were already mending. What he needed to do—and couldn't—was move. He had to get away from the hunters closing in on him. The poison-tipped arrows they used rendered dragons useless while still keeping their minds alert. But only for a short while. Given the chance, they would quarter him alive, and there was nothing he'd be able to do about it. He could only hope he'd flown fast and far enough to keep them from reaching him before he could defend himself again.

Once the paralysis receded, the hallucinations would begin. He'd no longer be able to tell friend from foe. Dragons—men of honor—had been killed to keep the rest of the clan safe from the ensuing rage after an attack. And the way his dragon had surged in defense of Stella when the bastards had threatened to kill her, he knew the fury inside him would explode.

All he could do was breathe through the pain, and hope time was on his side, and he survived the coming attack. It wasn't long before he scented the humans, so when leaves rustled to his left, followed by a snapping twig, he knew he was in trouble. Brycen tried to pick his head up off the ground, but it wouldn't budge.

The one Alexandra had named Trevor came into the clearing, his triumphant yell cutting through the quiet forest. He walked right up to Brycen's snout, nudging it with his boot. The bastard acted brave, but the sour smell of his fear filled Brycen's nostrils. He'd love nothing more than to whip his head up and chomp down on the coward. The fire in his gut built slowly, but it was coming. If by some miracle they didn't carve him up right away and make him bleed out, he'd be able to defend himself again, and soon.

The man sneered down at him. He angled his blade, lifting the edges of the scales at Brycen's neck and sliced through the tough hide beneath. Not enough to do any real damage, or kill him, but enough that he felt the warm trickle of blood down the side of his neck.

"You're not so tough, are you, dragon, now that you're on the ground at my feet?"

Fury roiled inside him as the man stepped back and laughed, turning to his friends, bright red dragon blood glistening on his sword.

Biding his time, Brycen concentrated on the anger, letting it build and churn until he had the strength to use it again. Already sensation was coming back. His arms and legs burned and tingled as feeling returned. Off to his right, the trees swayed from side to side as though dancing to some unheard music. *Shit.* Brycen closed his eyes for a moment, trying to dispel the vision. When he opened them again, the trees stood still. Giving in to the poison wasn't an option. He had to keep his head on straight. A few minutes that's all he'd have, so he had to make it count. Both his and Stella's lives depended on it.

Trevor didn't look back, in fact, none of them did. A mistake they would soon regret. Brycen took a steadying breath, testing out his strength with a quick flick of his tail. It moved. Not much, but it moved.

"Who wants to do the honors?" the man asked. "I'll take the female when she comes."

Rage, stronger than he'd ever felt blasted through Brycen. In an instant, power surged through him. He ignored the pain as he shot to his feet and roared. The men around him scattered, some running toward the treeline while others scrambled to find the bows they had dropped a distance away, but it was too late.

Brycen took several steps, and he was upon Trevor. The man swung his sword, slicing through the muscle and tissue on Brycen's chest, but nothing would save him. When the man lifted his arm to swing again, the sword undulated in a serpentine way that had Brycen blinking and taking a step back. The flash of pain to his right wing when the blade sliced through had him roaring, and fire spewing from his mouth. The man let out a blood-curdling scream as the flames engulfed him. Brycen didn't hesitate, clamping his teeth around the enemy's chest. He shook him from side to side until the screaming stopped, and the man lay motionless in his grip.

Heavy gusts of wind came at him from either side as two familiar dragons, one purple, one black, landed on the ground next to him. Working together, they found each hunter as they scattered and tried to get away. A few of them got as far as their bows, but none of them managed to get a single shot before one of the dragons was upon them. Only once their screams silenced, did Brycen face the other dragons.

Expecting to find his friends, he roared. Who the hell had fought with him? The black dragon had not one, but two heads. Luke didn't have two heads. The purple one shifted to the side, trying to get around him. He roared, warning them away. What did they want with him? Did they know about Stella? She-dragons, especially pure blooded ones, were rare. They had to be after her. Roaring, he stepped toward the black one. Dragon or no dragon, one head or two, he wasn't going to let anyone hurt her. When a sharp pinch stung his leg, he roared again, ready to eliminate the threat, but it was too late, the world around him melted.

***

Jace had come prepared, as he always did. Once Brycen had torn the hunters to shreds and had turned his fury toward his clan mates, he had been quick to stab him with the sedative that would allow him to heal and sleep off the hallucinogen. It needed to be done but damn it, that had left Stella alone for over two days. He couldn't catch his breath for the pounding of his heart. He flew fast and hard, not caring who was around. If the humans saw him and got scared, it was too fucking bad. He didn't care if he ripped his wounds open, or if his wing ever healed properly. All that mattered was getting back home to Stella. He should have fucking mated her when he'd had the chance, and begged forgiveness for not being more gentle with her. If she'd suffered through the change alone and wasn't able to shift back, he'd never forgive himself, and she wouldn't either.

He landed on the street, shifting as he ran across the lawn to his front door.

"Stella," he screamed the moment he had the door open. He tore through the house, only slowing long enough to glance in every room. "Stella, answer me, damn it!" When he found each room empty, a note in the kitchen with something illegible on it, and her dress still draped over the chair in his room, he roared.

"Shit. Where are you?" He grabbed the dress and brought it to his nose, inhaling her sweet scent. He didn't need the reminder of how delicious she smelled. He would be able to track her anywhere, but it made him feel better, so he sniffed again.

"Brycen! Jesus, fuck, man, you're going to kill yourself flying like that," Luke yelled.

Luke and Jace would help him find her. Luke was a damned fine tracker. They all were, but Luke was the best of the best. Between them, there was no way they'd lose her trail. He grabbed some clothes and headed back to the front of the house.

« CHAPTER 10 »

Blood soured the sweetness of Stella's scent, making Brycen's throat constrict. Small bloodied footsteps started a few blocks away, leading from the village center toward the outskirts. "She's hurt." Jace and Luke shared a glance, but neither said a word as they ran along with him. The footprints led to a small cottage. He didn't bother looking for a key when he found the door locked, choosing to batter it down with his sore shoulder instead.

"Stella!" He waited for her answer, but the house was silent. He was about to yell again when Jace rushed in.

"Neighbor says she left yesterday. Says she walked toward the mountains. The woman tried talking to her, but Stella just kept walking. She hasn't come back."

"Fuck." As pretty as the mountains behind her cottage were, they were treacherous to climb. He grabbed two shirts from her dresser and threw them at the men so they would have her scent. "I'm flying. Keep tracking from below. I have a feeling the dragon took her up high."

Brycen stripped and knotted his clothes, hanging them from his neck as he ran out the door, shifting before he even reached her front lawn. He couldn't care less if her neighbors saw him. He had to get to her, and fast. He left Luke and Jace to track on the ground, just in case his suspicion was wrong, and she had ended up in the forest instead of the mountain.

He'd searched three caves already, each one higher than the last, and hoped that he had finally found the right one.

"Stella," Brycen yelled as he shifted and ran into the cave. His heart hammered hard against his ribs. He had caught her scent about twenty feet down below. It was strong, maybe a little too strong. If she hadn't shifted yet, it wouldn't be long. *Damn it.* He couldn't be too late.

He rushed forward, not caring about the darkness. Once his eyes had adjusted, he'd be able to see as though it were the day. He listened for any sound to guide him to where she might be. "Stella! Answer me." It was so faint, he almost missed it, but a soft panting sound came from deep inside the cavern. Either he'd cornered a frightened animal, or Stella was still there.

Already he saw in shades of red. In another moment, he'd be able to make his way around with ease, but he couldn't wait. Stella needed him. He should never have left her alone. Had he let Luke and Jace take care of the conniving bitch, he and Stella would have finished their mating, and she wouldn't be in danger. Never again would he let anything or anyone get between them. That was if it wasn't already too late.

The scent of dragon filled the chamber. His jaw ached as he suppressed the need to shift—to go faster—but he held on to his control. He scanned the area, going from one side to the other, but she wasn't there. He was about to turn back when he heard the small whimper coming from a dark alcove against the cave wall. He was next to her in seconds. She lay there with her clothing neatly stacked to the side as though even the touch of material was too much for her tender skin to tolerate. Her chest heaved with her small pants. She was still in human form. There was still hope.

Falling to his knees beside her, Brycen brushed his fingers against her wet cheek. "I'm here. Please open your eyes for me, Stella." He pushed her long hair from where it partially covered her face, exposing her neck. Dark purple scales shimmered just beneath her skin, ready to explode to the surface.

She didn't respond, didn't acknowledge him at all.

"Open your eyes," he ordered. "Now." He hated being so harsh with her, but Stella wasn't in control anymore, the dragon was, and it wouldn't respond to sweet words and soft caresses.

The scales beneath her skin shuddered but did not recede.

"As your mate, I demand that you open your eyes and listen to me," he ordered again.

"I. Can't. Stop. It." The sultry smoothness of her voice was gone, replaced by a rumbling growl. When her eyes popped open, they flashed between brilliant blue to gold and back again. She was losing the battle against the dragon. They had to complete the mating ritual. Otherwise, she'd never be able to shift to her human form again.

"Listen to me, Stella. You're not doing this. You've held on this long. You can hang on for a few more minutes." He stood, and threw his bundled clothes next to hers. She looked up at him, and the shifting color of her eyes slowed so that they stayed blue for a few moments before going back to gold.

"That's right, sweetling. I'm here. Look at me. I'm going to take care of you." He knelt down and took her into his arms, and leaned his forehead against hers before standing again. "I'm so sorry. I shouldn't have left you. I won't make that mistake again. Not ever."

A spark of hunger burned in the gold depths of her eyes, sending burgeoning hope zipping through him. The dragon could be stubborn, and if she decided to refuse him, nothing he could do would make a difference.

Her eyes flashed blue again, and she pressed her lips to his, tentative at first, getting bolder as he tunneled his fingers through her hair and deepened the kiss. He turned her so that her back was against the smooth rock and wrapped her legs around his waist, pressing the length of his cock to her hot core. "Please, tell me you want this. Stella, I need to hear you say it." A pained expression crossed her features, and Brycen wanted to roar.

"I do. Please, make it stop," she whispered, her voice cracking a little.

"I swear I'll make this up to you," he promised. He positioned himself at her entrance and filled her with one hard thrust. He didn't budge for a heartbeat, reveling in the moist heat engulfing him.

Stella closed her eyes, moaning as he started to move. More than anything he wished he could have better prepared her, but they didn't have the time. He slid his cock out, only to drive it back in again, careful to keep her from slamming against the rock behind her. He'd never forgive himself if he hurt her any more than she'd already been.

The dragon inside him surged forward. His skin stung with the scales poking to get out. The small contractions already starting deep inside her had him moaning. Already too close to losing control, he pulled himself back, not enough to piss off her dragon, but to rein his in. He would have to take her like a fucking beast, but he'd hold on for as long as he could.

More than anything, he wanted her pleasure rippling through her as he laid his final claim on her. Neither his, or her, dragon needed it, but the human side of him did. Reaching between them, he circled her clit, stroking and teasing it as he continued pounding inside her. Her muscles rippled around his cock as she dug her nails into his shoulders, the sting bringing him closer to the edge. When he looked down, she had her eyes closed, and her mouth gaped open. Already, the shift had begun. Her teeth, usually perfectly blunt, had sharp, pointed tips. They could tear and rend—or mark her mate.

Brycen pulled her closer, pressing her against him. Her hardened nipples scraped against his chest, and he moaned again. Later he would ravish them along with the rest of her. He'd spend every day worshiping every part of her, but only if he could finish the ritual.

He tilted his pelvis, as he drove inside her again. A rumbling growl followed her soft keening wail. The dragon was close. His heart raced, and for the first time in his life, Brycen bared his neck to another dragon, getting no resistance from the beast inside him. This time, he would gladly take her bite. He would leave himself vulnerable to allow her to stake her claim.

"I'm ready to be your mate. Claim me, mark me as your own," he demanded as he kept thrusting into her.

The sharp edges of her teeth scraped against the skin of his shoulder, and he shuddered. His cock swelled inside her, and he was lost. Nothing had ever prepared him for the sizzling heat racing in his veins, or the pleasure streaking through him, as his dragon rose up to meet hers.

When she started to move with him, thrusting down onto him as he thrust up, his teeth pointed.

Stella half moaned, half growled when he removed his finger from her clit, but not for long as he gripped a handful of her hair in his fist. Her pussy clenched around him, so he tugged a little harder.

"Brycen..."

"Do it, Stella." He pounded harder and harder, scraping his knuckles against the stone behind her head with every thrust. He didn't care if he broke every damned bone in his hand, as long as when they were done, she was his—forever. Brycen tilted his head to the side again, exposing his neck. He hissed as her nails dug into the skin of his back. Faster, and harder, he drove into her. Each sexy whimper and growl slipping past her lips made his cock throb inside her. When her hot breath skimmed across his shoulder, he moaned and tilted his head a little more. He held his breath as the sharp points of her teeth pressed into his skin. One moment of scorching pain, then nothing but intense pulsing pleasure radiated from his neck and shoulder where she bit him straight to his cock.

Brycen didn't hold back—he couldn't. Harder and harder, he slammed into her, until her pussy quivered around him, tightening and releasing in spasms so tight, he could hardly stand it.

"Claim mate." His dragon roared into his mind. *"Claim her now."*

For once, Brycen had no desire to restrain the beast, and relinquished his control, knowing the dragon would take care of Stella just as surely as he would.

The moment Stella tore her mouth from his skin, Brycen tugged her hair, baring her neck, then claimed her as his.

Stella screamed as she shattered. Her pussy clenched and released him over and over. The pleasure rushing through him was more than he could take. When her orgasm started to wane, he thrust one last time, losing himself in her. He stayed there, with his teeth clamped to her neck, and her body wrapped around his for as long as he could, and would have stayed there longer had she not started wiggling beneath him.

« CHAPTER 11 »

Stella tried to move, but she couldn't. Brycen's body pinned her to the cold stone. As uncomfortable as she was, she couldn't help but smile against his neck. "I can't breathe," she wheezed out. "Maybe we can go home to snuggle?"

Brycen growled and nipped at her neck, a sweet, playful bite that had her heart racing and her body pulsing again. "I don't know if I can make it that far. How about if we change spots instead?"

He didn't wait for her to respond before he brought her down to the cave floor so that she was lying on top of him.

"There, much better." He slid his hand down her spine and back up again, his touch gentle, but purposeful. "Are you hurt?"

"No, I'm..." Deep inside, the dragon stretched and in an instant, it surged forward, stronger than ever. She thought that once mated the dragon would settle, but if anything, it seemed to be clamoring to get out even harder than before. Her skin itched all over and in her chest, heat churned, making it hard for her to breathe.

"Brycen?" She hated sounding so panicked, but what if the mating hadn't taken? She pushed up on his chest and looked at her arms. The scales were back, and try as she might to keep them from popping out, they came closer to the surface.

"It's okay. You'll be fine. I promise you." Brycen sat next to her, stroking a hand down her back again. "Let her come out, Stella. She just wants to explore her new world. We're mated now. You'll be able to come back."

"How can you be sure? What if she doesn't let me?" When he took her trembling hand into his, she gripped it tight. "Does it hurt? To shift, I mean?"

"My dragon connected with yours during the mating. She'll let you come back." He stroked a finger down her cheek and smiled. "It will feel odd, but it won't hurt. Just let it happen. The dragon knows what to do, and once you've done it, you'll want to do it all the time." He looked at her with a strange expression on his face. "How long have you been alone, Stella? You said you were the last of your line, when did the raid on your clan happen?"

Energy flooded her body, bringing a wave of heat with it. She stood, shaking her arms out as the tingling in them intensified. "T-twelve yea—" She gasped as a rushing sensation flooded her. "Brycen?"

"It's okay, sweetling. Just breathe through it," he assured her.

She took a deep breath, then another, welcoming the heat pouring into her rather than resisting it, and in an instant, raw power filled her. Although she saw well enough in the dark cave, her vision suddenly became crisp and clear. She saw every nook and cranny around her as though standing in the bright sunlight. Her skin tingled, an odd feeling, but not unpleasant.

With each breath she took, her body expanded and grew until she was looking down at Brycen, who now stood before her, smiling wide. A movement off to her right startled her, making her jump, and Brycen laugh. It took her a second to realize it was her flicking tail. When she looked at Brycen again, she opened her mouth to speak, but instead of words, a gurgling sound rumbled from her throat.

***

Beautiful purple scales shimmered over her body. Something about her shifted form was so familiar, but how could it be? Her dragon had never seen the light of day. When she opened her eyes, and a garbled croak came out, he couldn't stop the laughter from bubbling up. "You can't speak in this form, sweetling."

She brought her head down, and he couldn't resist stroking her smooth scales. "Stunning. You're just as gorgeous shifted as you are in human form," he said. "I wish we had a big mirror so you could see how beautiful you are."

She tilted her head to the side, trying to look at herself, then grunted when she couldn't quite do it.

The first time Brycen had shifted as a teen had been one of the best days of his life. The ultimate freedom, the liberation from being stuck in his human form, he hadn't ever wanted to shift back. Of course, as the day had worn on, and his energy had waned, he'd resumed his human form. But the rush, the exhilaration of shifting had never gone away. The fact that Stella had resisted her shift for so many years after adolescence showed just how powerful a bloodline she had.

"Let's get out of here," he said. Already his dragon was pushing to the surface. It had been patient so far, but it needed to shift—needed to be with its mate. "I'm a little bigger than you are, so you'll have to step to the side a little so we can both fit in here."

Once he had enough room, he let the change take him. The joy filled him as it always did, only, this time, it was deeper, richer. He wasn't alone.

He came close, stroking the side of her neck with his head, then almost purred when she returned the caress. With a gentle nudge, he directed her toward the cave entrance.

Brycen leaped from the rock-face first, roaring long, and loud, letting his clan mates know that he'd found her. If they didn't see the two dragons in the air, they would hear him and go home. There was no point in wasting their time climbing the mountain when he already had her safe and sound.

He flapped his wings, showing Stella that it was safe to jump. Her dragon didn't need instructions to fly, it was an ingrained ability just as natural as breathing, but having never done it, he figured she might be apprehensive. He needn't have worried. The moment he was in the air and turned to watch, she leaped after him. The dark purple of her scales sparkled in the sun. Stella flapped her wings in long, measured strokes as though she'd done it all her life. Flying high into the sky, she half-turned to look at him. That was when the shock of recognition finally hit him. He knew where he'd seen those scales before—those eyes. Where she had beautiful hair that looked like spun gold, Jace's was black as coal, but the eyes were the same, and so were the scales.

He had met Jace a few months after the hunters decimated his clan. They had both been alone, and so they had banded together, watching each other's backs while seeking revenge on those who had destroyed their families—their lives. Those bastards were dead, he and Jace had seen to that. The other eight Dragon Blood men had come along later, but they were as much of a clan now as any blood-related clan was, maybe more so for all the horrors they had survived together.

His heart pounded, and even though the dragon couldn't smile, inside, he was grinning like a fool. If his suspicion was right, he wasn't the only one whose life was about to change.

« CHAPTER 12 »

Everything Stella had gone through over the past few weeks, the fear, the frustration, the agony of her body's transformation, it all melted away. None of it mattered. In her wildest fantasies, never had she come anywhere close to imagining how wonderful soaring across the sky with her mate by her side would be. She glanced over at Brycen, who flew next to her. The same joy rushing through her shone in his eyes.

Through the eyes of her dragon, everything was sharper, clearer. The colors were brighter than ever before. She took a deep breath, and the smells of the forest down below came up to greet her. How could she have been part of the same world and not seen it the way she now did?

Far below a farmhouse with a big red barn looked small enough to be a child's toy, yet she saw it clearly. A dog ran across the yard, yapping at them as their shadows crossed the landscape. When she dipped in for a closer look, Brycen put on a burst of speed and flew beneath her, urging her higher once more.

She flapped her wings harder, cresting higher than she had before. Enjoying the rush as her body hurtled through the air. Muscles she'd never used before burned under the strain of flight. She never wanted to stop, but she was slowing. As much as she wanted to keep going forever, when Brycen turned them around and took her back toward the cave, she didn't resist.

The moment they got there, Brycen transformed. His shimmering blue scales shrunk and compressed until his skin emerged again. From start to finish, the whole thing took only a few seconds, but it had her heart racing. The smooth transition was as gorgeous as the man, and dragon were.

When she was done ogling him, she brought her human form to the forefront of her mind, willing the change, but nothing happened.

Brycen had said that the dragons had connected in their mating, and they had, but what if it hadn't been enough, or it had been too late? Her lungs burned, but she couldn't take a breath around the constriction in her throat. She pictured her blond hair, her eyes, her body, but still, nothing. A strangled sound rose from her throat. She was stuck.

"Stella, look at me," Brycen said as he stood in front of her. He waited until she locked her gaze with his. "You're fine, I promise. Take a couple of deep breaths, and try again. The dragon senses your fear. That's what's keeping you from shifting. She's trying to protect you. That's all."

Stella did as he asked, taking three steadying breaths in and out before bringing her human form into focus in her mind's eye again. This time, rather than think of the possibility of not being able to shift, she thought of Brycen standing there, waiting for her. Warmth flooded her body, not the searing heat like when she'd tried to suppress her first shift, but a soothing, calming presence. Her scales shivered and shook as they shrunk until they disappeared beneath her skin. Out of nowhere, her eyes watered and for some strange reason, she wanted to cry.

Brycen pulled her into his arms, stroking her back. "It was pretty intense, wasn't it?"

"It was amazing," she managed to croak out before the tears welled in her eyes again. "I never imagined it would be so beautiful."

"Let's get you home. As stunning as you were in your dragon form, and as delectable as you are now, I want to make love to you on a soft bed, not this cave floor."

Just the thought of hiking back down the mountain had her wincing and a shudder rushing through her. Her arms and belly muscles ached from exertion, not to mention her shoulders and back. Exhaustion beat at her. "I don't know if I have the energy to get back to Glen Farley." While she'd been in dragon form, the beast's power had kept her going, but now, her human body didn't want to move anymore.

Brycen smiled, his eyes sparkling. "If you can hang on, I can get us down there in a couple of minutes."

"You'll fly us down?" Already, her heart beat faster at the thought of soaring through the sky again.

He kissed the tip of her nose. "I will. But you have to get dressed. Just the idea of you riding me without a stitch on would be enough to make me crash."

She didn't waste any time arguing. The sooner she got her clothes on, the sooner they'd be flying again.

***

Stella bent over and picked up the clothing she'd folded and left on the ground, giving him a great view of her naked ass. It would be so easy to go to her, to kiss her, touch her, and make her his again, but Brycen held back. The dark circles under her eyes showed him just how tired she was. She needed food and rest, not a mate who couldn't keep his hands to himself. When she turned and faced him, he smiled. She was wearing his clothes again. Her tight little nipples poked at the fabric covering them. "I could get used to seeing you dressed in my stuff."

"I hope it's okay. When I left your house, I couldn't stand the thought of putting that dress on again, so I borrowed them."

If only she knew how much he loved seeing her small body inside his larger clothing, knowing what exquisiteness was hiding underneath. "It's fine. Borrow anything you like. As long as I get to take them off again, I'll be happy."

Stella licked her lips and took a step forward. "You want to take these off?" she suggested, running a finger along the V-neck of the T-shirt, pulling it lower, revealing mounds of soft, pale skin.

"I do, very much. But I won't, not now. Let's get you home, draw you a nice hot bath, fix you a meal, and then tuck you into bed. There will be plenty of time for me to ravish you once you've eaten and rested." He grabbed the jeans he'd tied up from the floor. "If you don't mind, we can tie this around your waist so you can hang on with both hands, and we can get out of here."

The flight to the base of the mountain was a short one. But when Stella squealed in delight as they took flight, he took his time, giving her a good view of Glen Farley and the surrounding farms. Cattle stampeded in the opposite direction when he got too close, but that only served to make Stella laugh, so he did it again. As a rule, he tried to stay away from the farms and the village in general while in dragon form. Not that it wasn't allowed, but it just made for friendlier neighbors when they weren't afraid of their livelihood being eaten by a hungry dragon.

He set down in a park not far from his house and waited for her to climb down before shifting again. She watched as he pulled his wrinkled jeans, and T-shirt on with a small smile on her lips, and her cheeks flushing pink. "Those beautiful eyes of yours are making promises the rest of your body can't keep." He came to her then and pulled her close. She didn't wait for him to kiss her. Instead, she pushed up on tiptoes and pressed herself closer as her lips met his. The kiss was soft and sweet—perfect.

"I wish I could argue, but I've never been this tired in my life," she admitted with a yawn.

Without another word, he scooped her up. She snuggled against him and rested her head on his shoulder, her warm breath teasing at his neck. "Close your eyes. We'll be home soon."

« CHAPTER 13 »

As tired as she had been when they had gotten home, Stella barely managed to eat half the meal Brycen prepared for her and fell asleep in the tub. She had planned to seduce him once they got to the bedroom, but her eyelids drooped, and her muscles wouldn't cooperate. When he didn't join her on the bed, she opened her mouth to protest, but another huge yawn came instead.

"Get some rest, sweetling." He eased her back down onto the pillow and brushed his lips against hers. "I have to make a phone call, but I'll be back soon."

When she woke next, the room was dark, and she nestled into Brycen's warmth, her back against his chest, and his large hand cupping one of her breasts. His soft snores ruffled the hair by her ear, and she smiled. She snuggled impossibly closer and drifted off to sleep again.

Stretching, Stella opened her eyes to a bright room. Sunlight filtered in through the open curtains. The spot where Brycen had been was empty but still warm. Following the sound of running water, she found him in the shower. He had already turned to block the spray and opened the door for her before she got there.

"Morning, beautiful," he said as he pulled her close.

She shouldn't be shy around this man. He was her mate, but still, heat rose up her neck and into her cheeks. "I'm sorry I slept so long."

"Don't be. You needed it. Your body has been through a lot in the past few days." He leaned in and pressed his lips to hers. "We're about to have company, one of the men in my clan, in fact, he might even be waiting downstairs as we speak, so we had better get a move on."

"I'm meeting your family today? You should have warned me. I have no clothes to wear." Her heart stuttered. What kind of impression would she leave with his clan if she paraded around the house naked?

"For starters, it's not family, not in the traditional sense. I lost mine in the raids, too. Second, you can wear something of mine. He won't care what you're wearing, and we'll go to your place and get your clothes later. Or I'll buy you a whole new wardrobe if you want."

"But—"

"But nothing. He will love you," he assured her. "His name is Jace."

A funny look flitted across his face, and then it was gone. She was about to ask him what was wrong when a male voice sounded from somewhere in the house.

"I'm here," the man announced, with a note of impatience in his tone.

"Oh, shit," she said. She looked up at Brycen, who just burst out laughing.

"You'll be fine. I promise. Finish your shower, and join us downstairs. I'll get started on breakfast." He gave her a hard, lingering kiss, then swapped places with her so that she was under the shower's spray. "Don't be too long."

Once he was gone, Stella steadied her nerves as she washed and rinsed her hair. When she got out, she found her bra sitting on top of a clean, white T-shirt, and another pair of sweatpants. These were a little smaller than the ones she'd worn before, but they were still too big. She tightened the drawstring as much as she could. At least they wouldn't fall.

She heard the male voices coming from the kitchen and stopped just outside to take a breath.

"I don't know, man. I'm not sure if it is now or not," Brycen said.

"What do you mean, you don't now? Last night, you sounded pretty damned convinced that she was my sister."

Stella didn't recognize the other voice, but a tingle went down her spine, and deep inside, her dragon perked up. *"Mine,"* it whispered into her mind, almost confused. Her heart pounded. They couldn't be talking about her. All except for her, the entire McLaughlin clan had perished over twelve years ago.

She took a shaky step forward, then another, until she was standing in the doorway. Neither of them had heard her silent, barefooted approach, neither looked in her direction. Brycen leaned against the counter with his arms crossed over his chest.

The other man, Jace, stood in front of him, his brows furrowed, and his hands stuck in his pockets. His hair, dark as the night sky, was standing on end as though he'd run his fingers through it. In profile, he looked so much like her father, only younger.

"I thought so, but—"

She must have made a sound, because right then, Brycen stopped talking, and both men turned to look at her. Jace stared at her, his mouth gaping open. His bright blue eyes a replica of her own. There was no way.

"Stella?" The man asked with a strangled voice.

She swallowed hard and nodded, unable to speak. In an instant, she was rushing past Brycen to the other man. Her vision blurred as moisture filled her eyes, then spilled down her cheeks. She didn't have to ask his name to know this was Jaceon. She had idolized her brother since the day she had been born. How could it be? Everyone had perished. He took her into his arms, hugging her so tight she could hardly breathe.

"I don't understand," she finally managed. "I thought you were dead. I stayed there for days, hoping that someone would come, but no one ever did. None of our hunters ever came back."

When he finally released her, he shook his head. "We were just entering the village when they came. They killed the others. I would have died too, had it not been for the old widow Morison. She found me and hid me in the forest. I was in bad shape. She managed to keep me alive. Once I was able to go back, there was nothing left. The whole village had been decimated."

"I know. I hid in the rubble when they came back to make sure no one had survived. I heard them laugh about how they killed us all." Before the pain she had managed to lock away for over a decade could swallow her whole, Brycen pulled her close, sharing her grief.

"There isn't anything we can do to change the past, but we have a lot to look forward to. Let's concentrate on that for now." Brycen said, pressing his lips to her temple.

Stella smiled up at him. Not only had she found her mate, but her brother, too. Nothing could take away the joy filling her, not the past, not the memories, and certainly not the bastards who had created them. Nothing. They would move forward and rebuild their lives, as a clan—as a family.

Her Gingerbread Dragon

Elianne Adams

http://elianneadams.com/

« CHAPTER 1 »

The cold northern wind cut through Luke Spence's jacket, pinching his cheeks. Stomping his feet, he brought feeling back to his frozen toes and shook the snow off his boots. His gloves were too thin, and of course, he hadn't worn a hat, but he didn't care. Under normal circumstances, he'd never choose to stand outside a baker's shop on such a frigid night, but this wasn't what he considered normal. Not by a long shot. Besides, he'd warm up fast enough once he was out of the cold.

When Stella had batted her eyelashes at him and begged him to run to the store for some eggnog, and nutmeg, he hadn't had the heart to say no. His best friend's mate had him—and all the other Dragon Blood men—wrapped around her little finger, and she knew it. In truth, he didn't mind the small favors she asked on occasion. Seeing Brycen so happy gave them all hope that they would find their mates eventually, too, which was why he had come out on such a blustery evening to begin with. Not in a million years had he imagined he would be standing outside looking through a store window with his heart racing as though he'd flown over the mountain at record-breaking speed, rather than sitting at the estate in front of a cozy fire.

He had just come out of the local grocery store when he'd caught a whiff of something sweet, savory, and so potent his entire body had reacted. Now that he'd caught the scent, he'd never forget it. One whiff, and everything else faded away. It wasn't the smell of sweet treats from the bakery that kept him rooted to the snow-covered sidewalk, but rather the scent of the woman who had waltzed past him and through the door, disappearing inside before he'd had more than a fleeting glance at her pink parka and fluffy white hat.

He was about to walk in after her when the cell in his jeans pocket buzzed. He thought of ignoring it, but knowing Stella, she'd forgotten something, and he sure as hell didn't want to make another trip into Glen Farley with the storm closing in. With his luck, he'd end up stuck in town. Dragon or no, flying in a blizzard like the one heading their way was ridiculously dangerous. As much as he loved the adrenaline rush, crashing into the mountain and spending the night buried in the snow freezing his balls off didn't appeal.

"Yeah," he answered with a smile. If he knew Stella, she was probably rolling her eyes at him, and would give him shit for not having better telephone manners when he got home.

"Luke, you still in town?"

His smile dropped a little when it was Brycen at the other end. He never called for the hell of it. "No, dude, I'm answering my phone mid-flight. Of course, I'm still in town," he replied. "What's wrong?"

"Nothing. Listen, Stella told me that she likes gingerbread. Think you can pick her up a little treat before heading back? I hear Johnson's Bakery makes great cookies."

Luke shook his head. Of course, Brycen would ask him to pick something up for his mate. The poor guy was still drowning in guilt over leaving her alone when she was about to shift for the first time. Had he not gotten to her in time, it would have been disastrous, but he had, and all was well. Of course, Stella had forgiven him right away, and the love that shone in her eyes each time she saw the man was there for all to see, but Brycen still wasn't over it. Maybe he never would be.

"I was about to head in there anyway. I'll see what I can find for her." At least now he had an excuse to go into the shop and stalk the woman who had his blood boiling hot in his veins. "Talk to you later."

The woman's sweet, spicy scent surrounded him the moment he opened the door. There was no denying it, this woman, whoever she was, was his mate. "Mate. Mine." the dragon's voice whispered into his mind.

"Yes, she is. But let's try not to scare her off. I don't think she's a dragon." He didn't think the beast would do anything to blow it, but the warning couldn't hurt.

The small shop consisted of a couple of tables with the chairs flipped upside down on top of them. The gangly teenager standing behind the counter rolled his eyes at him as he walked in, then looked pointedly at the clock. "We close in three minutes, mister," the kid said.

Luke couldn't care less about the kid, or the time the shop closed. Only two things mattered. Getting some gingerbread cookies for Stella, and getting closer to his mate. "I won't be long," he answered as he stepped up to the display case where the woman stood, not really looking at anything, but rather waiting for something.

"So what do you want, lady?" The kid asked, his tone as belligerent as his eye roll had been.

"I'm sorry, I didn't realize it was so late. Can I have three dozen gingerbread men, please?" The woman asked, her hands twisting the mittens she held in front of her. Her soft, lilting voice slid over him, making him want to growl, not in anger, but with the need rushing through him.

The kid rolled his eyes again and bent down to glance into the case. Luke looked into the display and his heart dropped. There was no way there were three dozen cookies left.

The kid shook his head and grabbed a box behind the counter. Throwing the cookies into the box, he counted out the twenty-seven gingerbread men, then filled the rest of the order with some white colored cookies. "There you go, lady."

Luke glanced in her direction, waiting for her to respond, but her face remained calm, and she smiled at the kid. She smiled. It wasn't until she handed over a twenty that he noticed the walking cane hanging from her right wrist.

Luke felt the blow like a punch in his gut. She couldn't see. Fury rose hard and fast. The kid was taking advantage of her. "Hey, kid, I think you made a mistake," he said.

"Mind your own business, mister." The kid glared at him, defiance radiating from the punk.

"And you're about to make another one." Luke stepped closer. "Miss, I'm sorry to intrude, but this young man hasn't given you three dozen gingerbreads, and he's about to shortchange you of five bucks."

The woman gasped and turned to face him, her lips forming a small circle. Her beautiful dark brown eyes shone with life, but stayed fixed. She didn't see him. "I... I... Thank you for telling me." She sighed and closed her mouth. Her bottom lip quivered for a moment, but then she squared her shoulder and faced the kid again.

"I expect that you will rectify the situation," she told the punk, her voice much cooler than it had been before. "I'll be speaking with Mrs. Bateman tomorrow. I'm certain she'll be interested to know that her employee isn't quite as trustworthy as she thinks."

"Listen, lady. I gave you three dozen cookies. I didn't have enough of the gingerbread. I was going to give you the right change. I made a mistake," the kid said as he glared at Luke again.

"Fine. I'll have my change now." She tilted her chin up and held her hand out in front of her.

Luke watched as the kid opened the register and got the correct change.

"I'm sorry, but we're closed now," the punk had the nerve to tell him as he slammed the register shut.

"No problem. I was looking for gingerbread, and it appears you're out." Luke shook his head and followed the woman to the door, reaching it before she did. "Allow me," he said, then opened it for her.

"Thanks again." She gave him a tight-lipped smile.

"Hey, can I interest you in a coffee or something?" he asked once they reached the sidewalk before she could walk away.

"Oh," the corners of her lips tilted higher, "I have to deliver the cookies first, but if you don't mind, a small detour, I'd love one.

« CHAPTER 2 »

What possessed her to say yes to coffee with a total stranger? Loneliness, that's what. Maddie hadn't even thought to say no, which was unusual for her in and of itself. And with good reason. The proof of how dishonorable people could be was steps away in the bakery. But there was something in the man's deep voice that had made her heart race a little, and her breath catch in her lungs. It didn't hurt that he'd called the young man at the bakery on his dishonesty.

"I'm Luke, by the way," he said from right next to her.

She jumped when the box she held was lifted and taken away from her. "I can carry the cookies," she replied. People were always underestimating her. Being blind sucked, but it was all she had ever known. Just because she couldn't see didn't mean she wasn't capable.

"Of course you can. And if you really want to, I'll give them back, but I was kind of hoping you'd take my arm. I like the idea of having your hand there. Call me old fashioned." He chuckled, and a funny little quiver rushed through her.

Heat raced up her cheeks. She was being silly. Not everyone out there was out to deceive or take advantage of her, just as not everyone thought her disabled. But many did. "No, it's fine. Thank you." She took a deep breath and reached out. His hand, much larger than her own, guided hers to the crook of his arm.

"I'm Maddison, but please, call me Maddie. Thanks for doing what you did in there. You have no idea how often things like that happen." She smiled up in his direction, then deciding to take advantage of having someone to walk with, she retracted her walking cane and stuffed it into her coat pocket. Something told her Luke wouldn't allow her to bump into things or walk into traffic, so she'd enjoy the moment while it lasted. It wasn't every day she was asked out for coffee, or anything else for that matter.

She wasn't foolish enough to go anywhere secluded with a total stranger, but there was no harm in going to the coffee shop. She knew Glen Farley well enough now. If he tried to pull her in the wrong direction, she'd know it. Besides, if she yelled for help in a small community like this, someone would come to her aid, wouldn't they?

"It shouldn't happen. Ever," he said, "but I'm glad I was there to prevent it this time," he said.

If the position of Luke's arm was anything to go by, he had to be close to six feet tall. "I know this makes some people uncomfortable, but if you don't mind, could you tell me what you look like?" She didn't beat around the bush. Unless he allowed her to touch his face, she'd never know, and she'd like to have a mental image of him in her mind while they spoke.

"I'm absolutely gorgeous. A hunk, really."

He laughed and she couldn't help smiling again. "I have no doubt."

"Okay, so, what should I tell you?" He hesitated a moment. "I have brown hair and brown eyes. I have a bit of a beard, also brown. I keep it short. It's due more to the fact that I don't shave every day than a desire to look like a lumberjack."

The picture she wanted started forming in her mind. How would that beard feel against her cheek... or more sensitive areas? "Is it rough? The beard, I mean?" The instant the words left her mouth, she regretted them. What kind of question was that? Certainly not one you asked someone you had just met.

He stopped walking and took her hand, then plucked her mitten off, and lifted it to his cheek. "Feel for yourself."

The cold wind whipped around her, and snowflakes melted on her cheeks, but right then, she didn't care. The heat radiating from his skin warmed her fingers. She slid her hand toward his chin, relishing the feel of the stubble on her palm. It was a little coarse, but not as much as she would have thought it might be.

A soft growl came at her, and she jerked her hand away. "Is that a dog?" It wasn't that she was afraid of dogs, but she steered clear of those that growled.

"It's okay. You're safe," he said, his voice soft and sure.

Luke slid her mitten back on, then placed her hand on his arm again.

"So, where are we off to? Or did you want to keep wandering down the street until we find someone looking for cookies?"

"Oh, we're heading to the Woolridge house on Pine. I can't remember the house number, but it's the fourth house on the right once we get there," she said.

"I'm familiar with the place. We're almost there already."

"I usually stay and visit with Gloria and Marybeth, but I'll drop off the cookies and we can be on our way." The spinster sisters would be disappointed, but she'd make it up to them the next time she brought something over.

***

Luke couldn't contain his smile. Maddie was bringing cookies to the Woolridge house. What he wanted to do was spin her into his arms and plant a kiss on her she'd never forget, but it was too soon. The way she'd pulled away when his dragon had surfaced and almost purred at her touching his face told him as much. He took a deep breath, inhaling her scent, savoring it. "I know the place. I've been there once or twice. If you want to visit with Gloria and Marybeth, we can do that instead of coffee." Of course, he wanted his mate all to himself, but he wouldn't put his own desires above hers, or the Woolridge's.

"No, I'll pop in on them tomorrow or the next day for a proper visit," she responded without missing a beat, making him smile even wider.

Maddie was stunning. Every part of her, well, what he could see that wasn't hidden under her thick winter coat, looked perfect. Her skin was flawless, smooth and creamy. He couldn't keep his eyes off her, when what he should be doing was watch that she didn't slip on a frozen puddle or trip over a crack in the sidewalk. Not that he could see the walkway for the snow accumulating on the ground, but still, it was his job as her mate to keep her safe.

"Have you always lived in Glen Farley?" He and the Dragon Blood clan had been around for a couple of years, yet not once had he set eyes on her, or caught her scent.

"I grew up in Denver, but I needed to get away from the craziness. As much as they have amenities for the blind, the hustle and bustle was getting to me, so here I am. I've been here for close to four months now."

"Ah, that makes sense. I moved out of the village half a year ago." He and his clan had purchased the estate on the mountain after Brycen and Stella were mated. There was no talk of little dragons coming yet, but they had all agreed a home away from people would be safer and easier to defend than one in the village. Besides, dragons weren't meant to live alone, and there was more than enough room for them all without getting in each other's way.

"So you don't live here?"

"Not in the village, no." He guided her to the walkway leading to Gloria and Marybeth's house. Already, he could hear the high pitched squeals of the children inside. "They knew you were coming, didn't they?"

Maddie laughed, and his whole body responded. The sound went straight down his body, igniting him from the inside out. "I may have mentioned bringing a treat over when I called earlier today."

By the time they delivered the cookies and fielded the questions coming from both Gloria and Marybeth, and had gotten hugs from all the children, the storm the weatherman had forecasted was upon them. The howling wind made any kind of conversation more than a little difficult. Luke put his arm around her shoulder, enjoying having her close even with all the layers of clothing separating them.

"Maybe we should take a rain check on the coffee. If you don't get started up the mountain soon, the road might be closed when you get there," Maddie suggested, her voice less chipper than it had been.

"You're probably right." As much as he wanted to spend more time with her, having her out in a snow storm had all his protective instincts screaming. He had to get her home safe. "Will you let me take you on a proper date, then? Once the storm passes?" he asked.

When she smiled and faced him, he had to fight from leaning in and kissing her. Every part of him wanted to—needed to—but he couldn't. Not yet. He settled for pulling off his glove and brushing a couple of snowflakes that had dared land on her cheek.

"I would like that," she said. "I should probably get home, and so should you. Will it be safe for you to drive up the mountain tonight?"

If he said no, would she offer him a place to stay? For half a second, he contemplated saying it wouldn't, but that wouldn't be fair. He'd have plenty of time with her once they were mated, and they *would* be mated. It was just a matter of time. "It'll be safe enough. Let's get you home, then I'll go."

"You don't have to do that. I can get there fine," she said firmly, but without the earlier defensiveness.

Should he push the issue? It had been clear when she'd objected to his carrying the box of cookies earlier that she valued her independence, and he respected that, but his protective instincts fought against reason. "All right, then." He shuffled his feet, not wanting to go, but knowing she expected him to.

Maddie's smile grew. "Don't you want my number or something? So you can call once the storm has passed?"

It hadn't occurred to him to ask for it. He would have found her regardless, but using the telephone made more sense. "Beautiful, and smart too, I'm a lucky man," he said, then pulled his phone out of his pocket. He glanced down at the screen. Three missed calls. "Okay, I'm ready."

She gave him her number and he programmed it in. "Perfect. Thank you."

"If it's not too much trouble, would you mind giving me a ring once you get home? So I know you made it there in one piece? I imagine you would have been there by now had you not spent the last hour entertaining the children with me, and I'd feel horrible if something happened and no one was out looking for you."

"I'll call." Who would have thought that having someone, other than his clan, worry about his safety, would fill him with so much joy? "In fact, it would set my mind at ease to know you've made it home safely as well." Not that he planned on leaving the village until she was safe indoors, but she didn't have to know that.

"Okay." She took a step back, then took her walking stick from her pocket, extending it with a quick flick of her wrist. "It was nice meeting you, Luke. I'll talk to you in a little while."

"Good night, Maddie." He watched her until she rounded the corner, before heading into an empty lot and out of sight.

It only took a few seconds to get rid of his clothes and place them with the eggnog, and nutmeg into the carrying pouch he had strung over his shoulder, and shift. In dragon form, the cold didn't sting quite as much. It wasn't that he liked it, but his higher body temperature tolerated it better.

Once up in the air, he found her about a block and a half away. Only after she was safe inside did he beat his wings harder and soar up into the sky, heading home.

« CHAPTER 3 »

Maddie pressed the button on her watch for the tenth time. Eight twenty-three, PM, the mechanical voice said. She groaned. Only six minutes since she'd last checked the time. She didn't know how long it would take Luke to drive up the mountain, but with the storm, he'd be taking his time. Still, each minute that went by without hearing from him had a dull ache tightening her neck and shoulders.

With the storm blowing in, it would take him a while to get home. Rather than sit there and worry, she headed into the bathroom and ran the water. A nice hot bath was what she needed. Although she had dressed well, the cold wind had chilled her to the bone. She might as well warm up while she waited for his call.

She hit play on her audiobook, and sighed as she sank neck-deep into the hot water, and the smooth voice of the narrator filled the room.

Closing her eyes, she took a deep breath, but rather than concentrate on the story, Luke crept into her mind again. Her fingers tingled at the remembered feel of his beard beneath them. The heat of his skin, even as they stood in the cold, had warmed her hand. His scent, something natural, almost wild, had made her mouth water for a taste of him. Her heart sped a little. She had heard that there we dragon shifters in the area, but she'd never met one before. At least, she didn't *think* she had. For all she knew, she could have walked by a fully shifted dragon and never known it. Could it be?

"Chapter four," The narrator announced. What had happened to chapter three? When she reached over to replay the story again, her phone rang. Water sloshed out the side of the tub as she jumped.

Three times the phone rang before she could get her hand on it and her finger on the right spot to answer. "Hello."

***

"Hi, Maddie, this is Luke. I take it you made it home safely after I left?" He knew darned well that she had, but he asked anyway.

"I did. I assume you've made it back up the mountain in one piece?" Her soft voice had his body hardening.

Her scent still teased his nose, and he had no desire to get rid of it.

"Just got in. I haven't even taken my coat off yet," he lied. The truth was, he went straight into the vestibule as soon as he got home and grabbed his phone even as he put his clothes on. He didn't even have his shirt on yet. Even though all of his pseudo brothers were used to seeing one another naked after shifting, they had started dressing before they entered the main part of the house out of respect for Stella.

"Well, don't let me stop you," Maddie said. "I'm sure you'll be anxious to get out of it and warm up."

Before he knew it, he was grinning like an idiot again. Maybe soon Stella wouldn't be the only reason the other men dressed before entering. His smile faltered as he remembered she wouldn't see them even if they entered in the nude. He pulled the phone from his ear only long enough to pull his shirt over his head, and managed two steps into the front hall before Stella was upon him.

"Luke, where have you been? I've been worried sick." She rushed over, eyeing him up and down.

He lifted his hand, showing her the grocer's bag, then indicated the phone in his hand. "Hang on," he told Maddie, who had gone silent.

"Sorry for worrying you. I had some pressing matters that needed attending." As much as he loved Stella, telling her about Maddie right then would only have her asking questions, and he would rather spend the time talking with his mate.

Stella gave him a squinted look, then chewed on her bottom lip. "Fine. Thank you for getting the stuff for me. I'm glad you're okay."

She came over and gave him a peck on the cheek, and he'd swear he heard a gasp at the other end of the line. Then sloshing water? He waited until Stella was heading toward the kitchen before speaking again.

"Sorry about that." Luke listened but heard nothing in the background over the phone.

"That's okay." Maddie's voice was much cooler than it had been.

"Is everything okay? You sound a little angry." Dare he hope she was jealous over what she had heard? He grinned again, waiting for her response.

"I don't know what you're talking about."

"Oh, so you didn't hear Stella speaking with me, or her kissing my *cheek*?" he teased.

She hesitated before speaking. "It doesn't matter. I'm glad you're home safe, I hope you have a good evening."

His smile dropped. He didn't want the conversation to end so soon. "Hey, wait. Aren't you curious about her? I mean, I did ask you out on a date a little while ago. Don't you want to know why there's a female kissing my cheek when I get home?"

She hesitated again. "I would, actually. I don't date men who are already involved."

His chest tightened at the thought of her on dates with other men. "Do you date often?"

"No, not often. Weren't we talking about your lady friend?" Maddie asked.

"Stella is a friend. Nothing more. She's my best friend, Brycen's... wife," he told her. He'd almost said mate, then thought better of it at the last second.

"And she's at your house?"

"She lives here, as do Brycen, and a bunch of other people. It's a sprawling estate with plenty of room for everyone. I'd love to bring you up here sometime. It's gorgeous and so peaceful." He closed his eyes and inwardly groaned. Of course, she wouldn't be able to see how beautiful their estate was or the views of the mountains from each window. "I'd be happy to describe it for you so you could get an idea of what it looks like," he offered.

"I'd like that, but would you mind calling back in a few minutes?" she asked.

Luke heard the distinct sound of water sloshing around again. "Of course. Is everything okay?" He listened again and the sound was gone.

"Yes, fine. I'm getting cold. I want to change and get comfy."

"Maddie?"

"Yes?"

His heart raced as he tried to keep his imagination in check. "Are you having a bath?" God above, he hoped so. Not that he could see her, but the idea of her naked in the tub and talking with him had his blood rushing through his veins and pooling in his groin.

She gasped and was silent for a few beats. "I... umm... I was cold when I got home, so I..." She sighed, and he held his breath. "Yes. I'm sorry, I shouldn't have answered the phone while I was in here," she said in a rush.

All the air rushed out of his lungs and a growl rumbled in his chest. "Don't apologize, Maddison. That's the sexiest damned thing I've ever heard."

Maddie's laughter came through the phone to ignite his blood even hotter.

"I'll give you ten minutes, then call back. Will that give you enough time?" he asked. He sure as hell hoped so. If he had to spend much more time than that imagining her naked, he'd be ready to fly back down the mountain to go to her.

"Yes, that's fine."

"Okay, I'll talk to you then." He waited for her to hang up before stuffing his phone in his pocket and heading toward the west wing.

"Did you get it?" Brycen hollered at him as he walked past the media room. Too preoccupied with thoughts of his naked mate, he hadn't even noticed him and Jace sitting in there.

"No. Sorry. They were out. My mate bought the last of them before I could get any." He said it so casually that neither of them said anything for a second.

"Damn. Thanks for trying... wait. What?" Brycen stood, his eyes rounded and his mouth gaped open.

"What?" Jace asked, having missed the whole mate thing.

"He just said his *mate* bought the last of the gingerbread cookies. I had asked him to pick some up for Stella while he was in the village," Brycen narrowed his eyes at him. "What mate?"

"I—"

"What are you guys talking about?" Stella came in with three glasses of eggnog and set them on the coffee table.

"Luke here was about to tell us about his *mate*," Jace explained.

"Your mate? I want to hear this." She clapped her hands in front of her and squealed. "I'm not going to be the only girl here anymore!"

"I met her tonight. That's why I was late coming back. Her name is Maddison. She likes to be called Maddie. She's absolutely gorgeous, and she's nice... and I need to call her again." He knew his smile was huge and the guys would bug the hell out of him for it later just as they'd done to Brycen for the past few months, but he didn't care. If he had a goofy look on his face half the time, he'd take it. "We're going to have to make some adjustments, though," he said as he started walking out of the room again.

"She's blind, so once she moves in here, we'll have to set things up so she can move around more easily. That is if she wants to move to the estate at all." He hoped she would, being without a clan for a few years before he had met Jace and Luke had been tough, but if she really wanted to live in Glen Farley, he'd live there with her. They could start their own clan, or even remain as part of Dragon Blood, but live apart. It would be different, not living with the people he now considered his family, but he'd adjust.

He didn't wait for them to ask any more questions before he turned toward his section of the estate.

"Wait, when do we get to meet her?" Stella hollered after him.

"I don't know," he yelled back, then laughed. "I still have to convince her that she's my mate."

« CHAPTER 4 »

As soon as she ended the call, Maddie let out a long sigh. What had gotten into her? First, she was jealous of a woman she'd never even met... over a man she barely knew, no less. Then she admitted to being naked in the tub while talking to him. If he turned out to be some creepy guy who wanted to take advantage of her, she'd given him plenty to think about, hadn't she? Thankfully, Luke didn't give her that vibe, and being blind, she considered herself to be a pretty good judge of character.

Tugging on the chain with her big toe, she pulled the plug and stood to get out. She wanted to be ready for when he called again. In her rush, she missed the mat. Her foot landed on the wet ceramic tile, and before she could stop her momentum, it slipped, sending her careening forward. Desperate to find something to grab a hold of, she whipped her arms out only to come up empty.

Her phone flew in one direction, and she went the other. Her heart plummeted at the splash she heard as it landed in the tub behind her. She fell forward, hitting her head on the corner of the sink.

When she finally got her feet under her again, her head spun a little, but she was okay. She reached for her towel to dab at the warm blood trickling from her forehead to her cheek. It didn't take long for the bleeding to stop once she applied pressure. With the tips of her fingers, she assessed the wound. Not too deep. She could disinfect it and put some kind of dressing on it for the night, then forget about it.

***

"Why the hell isn't she answering her phone?" Luke asked his empty room as he paced. It had been well over forty minutes since they'd hung up. She should have been dressed by then. Looking out the window, he couldn't see the peaks of the mountains for the snow that was falling. Not that surprising considering the forecast. He waited another two full minutes before hitting redial. Something was wrong. His gut told him as much. It was the same churning feeling that he got in his stomach as when hunters were near.

He waited, his fist tightening around the phone as it rang at her end, four, then five times before the answering service picked up again. "Hey, Maddie, it's

Luke. Listen, I don't want to be a pain, and if you aren't interested, it's okay, but please, if you can, answer the phone to let me know you're okay." It wasn't, and there was no way he'd let her go without trying to win her over, but he had to know she was all right. He hadn't left a message the first ten times he'd called, but if she didn't answer soon, he was heading back to Glen Farley. To hell with the storm.

He tossed the phone onto his bed and grabbed his bag before heading to his closet. If he were going back to the village, he wouldn't be able to make it back to the estate in the storm. Hell, he'd be lucky to make it to Maddie's in one piece. He'd have to check into a sleazy motel for the night, or beg for a spot on the Woolridge couch. Then again, considering the interrogation he'd have to face there, he'd rather stay at the motel.

He was going to try ringing her one more time. If she didn't answer, he was going down there. For all he knew, she could have lost power in the storm and was stuck at home alone with no heat. Not that he could do a whole lot to restore power, but at least he could supply heat so she didn't freeze to death.

When the ringing stopped and he got her voicemail again, he grabbed his bag and headed for the door.

"Hey, where are you going? In case you hadn't noticed, the blizzard is in full swing." Jace stopped him before he reached the door.

"She's not answering her phone," he said, then huffed when Jace looked at him with a blank expression. He glanced at his watch. "Maddie isn't answering her phone. I told her I'd call her back in ten minutes, but she's not answering."

"She probably fell asleep or something. There's no point in getting yourself killed."

Luke wasn't about to tell Jace that she had been in the tub while they'd been talking. "No. Something's wrong. I can feel it."

Jace's eyes narrowed. "Hunters?" he asked, then continued without waiting for the answer. "I'll come with you. Give me a sec to tell Brycen and Austin. The others are on assignment, but we can call them back."

"Wait. No. Sit tight." He loved that his clan always had his back, but he wouldn't put anyone in harm's way until he knew there was a need for it. "I'll call for backup if I need it once I get there."

Jace didn't look convinced, but he nodded. "Call even if there's no trouble. You won't make it back up here tonight. Stella will worry."

Luke grinned. "I know. I'll call."

It didn't take him long to undress and loop his pack around his neck. The moment he was in the front yard, he shifted and was up in the air again.

Under normal circumstances, he could fly down to the village in less than ten minutes, but he couldn't see more than a few feet in front of him. The dragon was restless, but even he knew he had to take it easy. He wouldn't be of any help to Maddie if he crashed into the side of the mountain. When he finally saw the lights of the houses below his muscles loosened up a little, but then why hadn't Maddie answered her phone?

He circled her block once before landing in her neighbor's yard. The lights were on in all but two windows in the small apartment complex she had gone into earlier. Although the dragon provided plenty of heat, the biting wind pinched at his skin. Grabbing his jeans from his bag, he pulled them on. There'd be time to put his socks and underwear on once he was someplace warmer. He had pulled his sweater over his head when the porch light flicked on.

"What are you doing back there?" An elderly man peered out his back door, then shook his head. "Damned dragons, always trampling over my lawn," he grumbled before he turned and slammed his door behind him.

Did the man not see the blanket of snow covering his precious lawn? By the end of the week, it would be more than flat, it would be frozen solid. Luke slipped his wet feet into his sneakers, then grabbed his things and headed to the sidewalk. He didn't stop until he was inside Maddie's building, and then, only long enough to catch her scent, directing him to the right apartment.

Luke had his hand up to knock when Maddie's scent, mingled with a familiar coppery smell reached him. Blood. He knocked on the door, rattling the welcome sign hanging there. When he didn't hear anything right away, he pounded again. *It's probably nothing. Take it easy, Luke.*

"Hold on." Maddie's muffled voice came through the door.

He released the air he hadn't realized he'd been holding and took a deep breath, easing the burn in his lungs.

Her footsteps stopped on the other side of the door. "Who is it?" she asked.

Luke closed his eyes and took another slow breath. "It's Luke." Smart woman, she hadn't opened the door without checking first.

"Luke?"

He heard the rattle of a chain lock, then not one, but two bolts clicking before she finally opened the door.

"What are you doing here? I thought you went home?"

His relief at seeing her standing there died fast when he saw the bandage with blood seeping through on her forehead. "I did. What happened?"

Her cheeks grew red. "I fell while getting out of the tub."

"Shit. Are you okay?" He took a step closer, reaching out for her, but then dropped his hand. "Can we go inside?"

"I'm fine. Why are you here, Luke? How did you get home and all the way back to the village in the storm? I would have thought the roads would have been closed by now."

She was going to be pissed, but he had to tell her. "Let's go inside and I'll answer your questions."

She hesitated, but then nodded and turned, leaving him to close and lock the door.

She waited for him at the end of a small sofa. "Have a seat. Can I get you something to drink?" she offered.

"No, I'm good. Thanks, though." He took her hand, keeping her smaller one in his as they both sat. "Before I say anything else, I want you to know that you're in no danger from me. I would never hurt you in any way, or take advantage of you."

Her eyes narrowed. "Okay."

"Maddie, I'm a dragon shifter. I made it up the mountain and down again so fast because I flew there and back. I didn't drive. I have no idea if the roads are closed or not. I seldom use them."

Maddie gasped, but didn't pull her hand from his. "I knew it."

She smiled, and the rest of the tension drained from his body. She hadn't pulled away or freaked out. Maybe convincing her to give them a chance wouldn't be as tough as he had feared.

"So why are you here, Luke? How did you find me?"

The muscles in his shoulders tensed again. "I flew overhead and made sure you made it home safely earlier. That's how I found your apartment building. Once inside, I used my nose to find you," he said in a rush. He didn't know Maddie well, but he knew she valued her independence.

She worried her bottom lip between her teeth for a moment. "I made it home safe and sound."

"I know," he said.

"I don't need to be coddled or protected. I manage quite well on my own," she insisted.

"I figured as much."

"So why follow me home? Why come rushing back down the mountain in a blizzard?"

With her eyebrows drawn, she looked so cute he wanted to kiss the frown from her lips, but he settled for smiling even though she couldn't see him. "I needed to make sure you made it home safe. It had nothing to do with you being blind. I would have done the same thing had you been able to see." And he would have. Any self-respecting dragon ensured their mate's safety.

She nibbled at her bottom lip again and he had to swallow his groan. Everything she did was so damned sexy.

"But why?" she finally asked.

His stomach plummeted. Of course, she'd keep asking. "I'm not going to start our relationship with lies, Maddison. I did all that because you're my mate."

Her eyes grew wide and she opened her mouth to say something.

"Before you shoot the idea down, hear me out. Dragons aren't the same as humans. Our bodies, while in human form are quite similar, and function pretty much the same way, but the dragon is not the same. The dragon feels and senses things that humans can't. It knows its mate by scent. The chemical reaction in my body doesn't lie. I knew you were mine the moment you walked past me to go into the bakery. So yes, even though you are capable and independent, I had to see you home safe. The dragon wouldn't allow anything else even though in my mind, I knew it wasn't necessary."

"Oh." She pulled her hand from his and stood. She took a few steps away, avoiding the coffee table entirely before turning toward him again. "So what does that mean?"

Luke wanted to eat up the few short feet between them and have her near again, but he stayed where he was. "It means that you're the one who was meant for me. No one else could come close to having the same effect on me as you do. And it's more than physical attraction though I'll admit, that's there in a huge way. It's a soul bond, something that can't be broken."

« CHAPTER 5 »

Holy crap. She was his mate? Maddie's heart pounded. She didn't know if she should laugh or cry. There was something about Luke that drew her to him, there was no doubt about that, but his mate? When he was close, her whole body settled. It was like she didn't have to be hyper vigilant with him around. He'd look out for her. But at the same time, a different kind of tension coiled. The longer she spent in his presence, the closer she wanted to get to him. She'd never had such a physical, visceral reaction, to a man before, and truth be told, it scared her a little.

"Maddie," he spoke, breaking her out of her own thoughts.

"Yes?"

"There's nothing to worry about here. I'm not going to push you for more than you're willing to give. I didn't tell you all that so that you feel pressured."

The material of the couch cushions scraped against his pants as he stood. He took two steps toward her, but she didn't back away.

"I didn't want dishonesty between us," he said from right in front of her.

"So now what?"

"Now, you let me look at your wound to be sure you're okay, and then I'll go."

The heat emanating from his body warmed her skin. He was close. His scent enveloped her and she took a deep breath, wanting more. "It's fine. I promise."

"I'm sure you're right, but blood is seeping through, and the dressing needs to be changed anyway. I really don't mind doing it," he insisted.

"The first aid kit is in the bathroom." She tried to turn to go get it, but he put his hands on her shoulders, stopping her.

His breath fanned her cheek. He was so close, if she turned, she was sure her lips would meet his. "I can get it if you like," he offered.

"No, it's okay. I'll be right back." This time when she turned, he let her. She didn't have to see to know that he followed her with his gaze. The tingle racing through her said it all, and if it made her put a little extra sway to her hips, then so be it. Whatever it was that pulled her to Luke was getting stronger, and she had no desire to fight it. When she got to the door leading to the hall, she turned and smiled at him. "Thank you for coming to check up on me, Luke. I appreciate it."

Now that her head had stopped spinning, she might as well rescue her phone while she was in there. She steadied herself, making sure of her footing before she bent down to retrieve it. Sweeping her hands along the bottom, she came up empty. She tried again, twice, but still, nothing. If she didn't come back out soon, she was sure Luke would come in after her, so she might as well call him in.

"Luke?"

She heard his footsteps coming toward her in an instant. "Are you okay?" he asked. His breath hissed out of him as he rounded the corner.

She straightened, blushing. She hadn't even thought of the sight she'd make bent over the tub that way. "When I fell earlier, my phone went flying. It landed somewhere in the tub, but I can't seem to find it."

"Here, let me." He squeezed in behind her, resting one hand on her hip as he reached down. "I don't think it'll work again, it's full of water."

His voice was hoarser than it had been before, and his fingers tightened on her hip. When he shifted to his other foot, she couldn't help but feel the heat of his body all along the back of her legs and back.

"Here," he said, placing her dripping wet phone in her hand.

"Thank you. Since you're here, maybe we can change the dressing here?" She turned, brushing up against his hard body before sitting on the edge of the tub.

"Sure, whatever you want." She heard him rifling through the first aid kit for a moment before he started pulling at the tape holding the old bandage in place. "You've got a bit of hair stuck in the tape. I'll try not to pull it."

"Thanks." With his scent, and his warmth surrounding her, she could hardly think, much less speak.

"There we go. The cut is clean, but I'll disinfect it again to make sure. You're going to have a nasty bruise on your forehead for a few days. It doesn't need stitches, but I'll have to realign the skin a little so you don't end up with a scar."

He was so gentle with her that she hardly felt a thing. It didn't take long that the wound was cleaned and he had a new dressing covering it. "Thank you. Now will you kiss it to make it better?" she teased. Expecting that he'd step away, she stood, only to find that he was right there. In an instant, his hands tilted her face to his, and his lips descended on hers.

She stood there for a moment, too shocked to do anything else, but when his tongue probed at her seeking entrance, she let him in. He tasted as delicious as he smelled, and she couldn't get enough. She wrapped her arms around his neck, drawing him closer.

A soft growl rumbled in his chest—against hers, making her nipples pebble with the vibration. His arms came around her, wrapping her in his strength. Every part of him was hard, well defined, and pressing against her. When he finally loosened his hold, and maybe thought of pulling away, she dug her fingers into his hair and brought him back for more.

"Luke," she whispered when she finally pulled her lips from his.

He groaned and his arms tightened around her until she could hardly breathe. What was she doing? She was kissing a man she'd only just met right there in her bathroom as though she'd known him for years. That wasn't her. She wasn't so trusting.

When his mouth grazed her cheek, heading to her lips again, she brought her hands to his chest, pushing with enough pressure to stop him.

"I'm sorry, give me a minute." His breath teased at her ear with each panting breath he took as he held her close. His heart pounded hard enough that she felt it where her breasts were mashed against him.

A deep shudder rushed through him. Was he okay? "I'm sorry. Things were moving a little too fast." She brought her hands up his shoulders, then pulled back to cup his cheek. The skin beneath her palms was rough. Hard even. Startled, she tried to take a step back, but she was up against the tub. Had his arms not been around her still, she would have tumbled for the second time that night.

"You're safe, Maddie. Even if the dragon comes forward, it would never hurt you, just as I wouldn't," he assured her.

She nodded, and swallowed hard, her mouth suddenly dry.

"I should go."

He let his arms drop and took a step back. Part of her wanted to step forward and pull him close again, but she couldn't. She had to think—to breathe. "Is it safe to fly? With the storm, I mean?"

"Not likely, but I wasn't planning on going back tonight anyway."

Gasping, Maddie crossed her arms over her chest. He'd been presumptuous thinking she'd welcome him into her bed so soon, hadn't he?

"I meant that I was planning on heading over to the Old Time Inn and getting a room until the storm blows over." Luke's deep, rich laughter flooded the room. "Not to say I don't like where your mind was heading, but maybe we can get to know one another better first."

Heat rushed up her chest and neck to settle into her cheeks, but by the time he stopped laughing, she was giggling too. "That's probably a good idea."

He stroked her cheek with his knuckles, and she leaned into the caress. "I really should go and let you get some sleep."

She followed him into the living room, an uneasy feeling settling in her stomach. She stood next to the couch as his footsteps took Luke closer to the door. "Wait. What if the Inn is full? It's usually booked solid when the weather gets bad."

"I'll be fine. Worst case scenario, I'll ask Marybeth, and Gloria if I can crash at their house."

The Woolridge's didn't have a spare bed with all those children they were fostering. They barely had enough room for the people living under their roof as it was. "Call the Inn and see if they have a vacancy before you head out into the cold. I'd feel better knowing you weren't stuck in the snow."

She heard some rustling, then silence for a while, before finally hearing the telltale beeps of a cell phone being dialed. She listened to the short conversation, her heart racing a little. "That's that. You have to stay here," she blurted out before she could lose her nerve.

"Maddie..."

"No, I mean it. I want you to stay. I don't have a spare bedroom, but I can sleep on the couch since I'm shorter than you are. You can have the bed." The idea of snuggling between her sheets and having his scent all over them for the next few days sent little butterflies fluttering in her stomach.

« CHAPTER 6 »

Luke watched as Maddie nibbled on her lower lip. She had a habit of doing that, and each time she did, need pure, and hot, rushed through him. What he wanted to do was pull her into his arms and kiss her senseless again, but that was a bad idea. He was the one who had lost his head when he'd kissed her in the bathroom, and his dragon had surged forward. There had been no real danger of him shifting, or the dragon gaining any true control, but Maddie hadn't known that, and feeling the dragon so close to the surface, had frightened her.

The fact that she had invited him to stay with her gave him hope that he hadn't quite blown it, so he sure as hell wasn't going to do anything to make her pull away again.

"If I stay, it'll be on the couch, or on the floor if I need to stretch." Heaven only knew he'd slept on worse. Caves and rocky cliffs didn't offer much in the way of comfort, but they were generally a safe place for a dragon to sleep. "If you'll tell me where to grab a blanket, I'll get settled so you can get to bed. It's getting late."

Her hand went to her wrist, and with the push of a button, a mechanical female voice rose from her watch. "Eleven forty-eight, PM."

"I hadn't realized the time. Umm... if you go back into the hallway, there's a closet with some blankets and pillows. I really don't mind the couch, though—"

"I appreciate the offer, but no." Before she could protest again, he went and grabbed what he needed. Considering the heat his body naturally produced, chances were slim that he'd use a blanket, but he took one in case.

"I guess I'll turn in then. Is there anything else you need before I go to bed?" she asked when he entered the room again.

"No, I have everything I need. Thanks for letting me stay, Maddie." There wasn't anywhere else on earth he would rather be. If he had to sleep in the hallway guarding her front door, he would have done so willingly, but he wasn't about to tell her that.

***

Unable to find anything else to stall with, Maddie took the few steps separating them. The soft stubble tickled at her lips as she stood on tiptoes to kiss Luke's cheek. "Thanks again for coming to check on me tonight. I'm glad you did," she admitted, then stepped around him and down the hallway to her room.

As tired as she was, she didn't bother listening to a chapter of her book before settling into bed.

His hot, spicy scent lingered on her skin. She brought her fingers to her lips, remembering the feel and taste of him. Boy, the man could kiss. She didn't have a ton of experience with men, but what she did have paled in comparison. She settled more deeply beneath her covers, forcing her thoughts away from the man in her living room. Of course, it was impossible. As soon as one thought left her mind, Luke filled it again.

His mate. Never in a million years had she considered that she might be a dragon shifter's mate. She'd always dreamed of finding a good man to love and grow old with, but a dragon? Not that she cared that he was a shifter, but it did complicate things. Most people were very accepting of the species, and even welcomed them into their communities, but that wasn't true of everyone. Dragon hunts still happened. In fact, she'd heard that one had happened not far from Glen Farley last summer.

Maddie gasped, and sat bolt upright. Had Luke been in danger? If she remembered correctly, one dragon had been hurt. With her heart racing, she settled back into bed. She'd have to remember to ask him about it in the morning. Not that it would change the past, but she needed to know how safe it was for him to live in the area and how much danger he faced on a regular basis.

She tossed and turned, finally drifting off into a fitful sleep. When dreams of innocent dragons being hunted by ogres tore her from her sleep, she pressed the button on her watch. *"Four Twenty-One, AM."* Her apartment was cold... and quiet—too quiet. She couldn't hear the soft whir of the fan she used year round in her room. The power had to have cut out. She shivered and shook, her teeth chattering. The tip of her nose was like ice. If she was that cold under her thick comforter, Luke had to be freezing in the living room.

As much as she hated to get out from under the covers, she tossed them to the side and slid her feet into her fuzzy slippers. Not having lights was not a problem for her, but if Luke had to get up to use the restroom, he might have issues. She stopped at the closet on her way to the living room, grabbing an extra blanket and a flashlight. She'd come close to throwing the flashlight out more than once while cleaning, but she was glad she hadn't. Now she had to hope that the batteries still had enough power to make it work.

The sounds of Luke's long, deep breaths met her when she entered the living room. She'd put the extra blanket on him and leave the flashlight on the table next to him. Hopefully, he'd find it if he woke before it was light out. Unfolding the blanket, she reached and covered him from his feet up to his chest, but before she could pull away, his warm hand wrapped around her wrist.

"What a beautiful sight to wake up to," he said, his voice low and raspy from sleep.

"Oh," she tried to pull her hand away, but he held her there, not tightly, but enough to keep her where she was. "I didn't mean to wake you. The power went out, and it's getting cold in here. I wanted to give you an extra blanket."

He pulled her a little closer, then placed her hand on his naked chest. "Dragons tend to be warmer than humans. I'm not cold, but your hand is like ice. How's the rest of you?"

For once, she was glad for the darkness. He wouldn't see her blush. Having her hand on his chest was making her hotter than any blanket could. She hadn't moved her hand from where he'd placed it to explore more, but what she did feel was hard and muscular. She could only imagine how the rest of it would feel under her fingers. And he was right, his skin was warm.

"I'm a little chilled, but I'm sure I'll be okay until morning. I have more blankets I can pile onto my bed." She pulled her lip between her teeth and flexed her fingers a little, and Luke moaned. The soft, rumbling sound sent heat rushing through her body. She gave her hand a little tug, and this time, he let her go. "I'm sorry. I shouldn't have done that."

"Don't be sorry. You're more than welcome to touch any part of me at any time, Maddison."

She heard him shifting on the couch. He wrapped an arm around her back in an odd kind of hug.

"I won't let you fall," he said, then in the next instant, he stooped down and lifted her into his arms.

She couldn't keep the small squeal from slipping past her lips. She hadn't been carried since she had been a child, but he held her against him, secure in his arms. "What are you doing?" she asked, the breathlessness in her voice caused more by his nearness than the sudden movement.

"I'm taking you back to your bed." Luke laughed, then nuzzled her neck. "You smell so damned good, Maddie."

"I... uh, thank you." What was she supposed to say to that?

"Your slippers are adorable, by the way." He started walking, and she stiffened.

"Wait, there's a flashlight on the table. I don't want you to run into anything and give me a concussion."

Luke laughed again. "Seeing in the dark isn't a problem. I can see almost as well as in broad daylight, so you don't need to worry about me slamming you into a wall, or a chair, or anything else for that matter."

"Oh."

He started walking again, not stopping until he was in her room. He placed her gently on the bed, before pulling the blankets up to her chin. "I'd like to sleep in this bed with you if you'd let me," he said. "I promise I won't try anything. I won't even touch you if you don't want me to, but my body heat will keep you warm for the rest of the night."

Maddie's breath caught in her throat. She didn't know Luke, but the idea of freezing for the next few hours didn't appeal to her at all. Not to mention the fact that part of her really wanted him to stay. "Okay, but only to sleep," she said before she could chicken out.

His padded footsteps went around the bed to the other side. His weight made the mattress dip, then with a couple of pulls on the blankets, he was lying next to her. He scooted close enough for his warmth to tease her skin. "You can get closer if you want. I won't touch you unless you want me to, so if you want to get warmer, you can snuggle in. I'd love to hold you while you slept, but I'll keep to my side if that makes you more comfortable."

Another shiver raced over her skin. She couldn't tell if it was due to his proximity or the temperature in the room. She nibbled at her lip before scooting closer. He wrapped his arm around her shoulder, pulling her into his side. After a moment, she took a deep breath, and settled into his heat, resting her head against his shoulder.

"Wow, you really are cold." Luke laughed, but then he took her hand and placed it on his belly, covering it with his much warmer one. "There. You'll be toasty in no time."

Long after Maddie drifted off to sleep, Luke stayed there, wide awake. Never would he have imagined the peaceful feeling of lying there with his mate in his arms. Sure, he was too warm, but he wouldn't trade being there with her for anything. He hadn't fully understood Brycen's goofy looking smiles, or his annoying habit of dropping everything to go check on Stella, or to go see her in the middle of the day until then. Maddie could ask him for anything, and if it were within his power to give it to her, he would, no doubt about it.

She wiggled against him in her sleep, then draped her flannel covered leg over his, pressing up against his already aching groin in the process. Stifling his moan, he let her settle again and pressed his lips to her soft, silky hair. What the hell was he going to do, when she expected him to go back home, and she stay at her apartment? Living apart until she was ready to be his mate in every sense of the word would kill him, he just knew it. His arm tightened around her, and he had to forcibly relax it when she stirred.

He kept his breathing deep and steady, so when she nuzzled his chest with her cheek, then smiled against his skin, she didn't pull away. Her hand, which had been resting on his stomach came up to his chest, caressing him with a feather-light touch that made him want to moan, but he kept it inside. Her innocent exploration had blood rushing hot in his veins to pool in his groin. If her thigh were another inch higher, she'd be sure to feel it, hard and ready for her. But he'd promised to keep his hands to himself, and he wasn't going to break it. He'd be enjoying her gorgeous body soon enough.

« CHAPTER 7 »

Maddie stretched as much as she could with Luke wrapped around her. At some point while they slept, she'd turned onto her side, and he had followed, surrounding her in warmth. True to his word, he hadn't made any advances, further proving that he was trustworthy. Heat rushed into her cheeks as she remembered waking and feeling his chest while he slept. Had it not been so risky, she might have gotten bolder. She had wanted to touch every part of him, a reaction that took her by surprise, but she held herself in check. Imagine him waking up to find her groping him in the middle of the night. He would have wanted more. Would that have been such a bad thing?

If her internal clock was working, and it always did, it was close to time for breakfast. Too bad it was so cold in the apartment. She didn't want to leave the bed. Luke had kept her comfortable for the few remaining hours of sleep they had gotten, but slipping out from beneath the covers would be brutal. It wasn't like she could cook him breakfast anyway. Maybe he'd like some cereal? She dismissed the thought. She doubted she had any cereal in the cupboard. She tended to eat more protein, fruit, and veggies, so she didn't keep a lot of that stuff around.

Luke took a deep breath and pulled her closer to his chest. "Good morning, gorgeous," he said, his voice deep, and drowsy, and sexy.

"Good morning." She snuggled closer, then gasped at the solid feel of his cock pressing against her bottom.

"It's okay, I won't do anything with it. It's just as happy to see you this morning as the rest of me is." He rubbed his beard against her neck.

Her nipples pebbled beneath her shirt, and a pulse throbbed between her thighs. She may not have known Luke for long, but what she did know of him, she liked. "Maybe I want you to do something with it." She twisted in his arms so that she faced him.

He held her for a few moments in silence. "I don't want you to feel like you have to, Maddie. I'm perfectly happy holding you, and spending time with you—getting to know you."

Being so close to him, she didn't want to discuss things anymore. Leaning in, she pressed her lips to his. He didn't respond for a beat, then he moaned. He brought his hands up her back to her neck, holding her in place as he kissed her. His tongue slid between her lips, and it was her turn to moan. His taste, his scent, everything about him appealed to her. She pressed her body into his, and caressed his chest as she'd done during the night, loving the tremor that coursed through him at her slight touch.

His cock, hard and insistent against her thigh jerked when she brought her hand lower to trace the waistband of the jeans that covered him from the waist down. He broke the kiss then, "Maddie," he said, his voice strangled.

"I'm certain, Luke. I want this. Don't you?" she asked, knowing without a doubt that he did.

"More than anything. But I don't want you to have regrets."

"I won't," she assured him, then kissed is collarbone. She grazed her teeth there, then moved lower to circle his nipple with her tongue.

His breath hissed out from between his teeth. When she finally flicked her tongue over the hardened peak, she gasped at the cool ring she found there. "Luke?"

"It's a nipple ring, it makes me super sensitive there."

"How come I didn't feel it last night?" Heat rushed up her cheeks, and she tried to hide her face in his chest as the realization of what she'd admitted dawned on her.

"Because last night you were trying not to wake me, and didn't get close enough to my nipples to find them."

"Them? There's two?" Another wave of desire pulsed through her. She'd never been with anyone with nipple rings before. She pushed away from him a little. "And you were awake?" she accused.

"I was, and I told you before, you can touch every part of me anytime you want. I won't stop you."

She fingered the little ring on his nipple, smiling when he moaned again. "Every part?"

"Yes," he moaned the word out when she flicked it again.

"Even here?" She slid her hand down his belly, not stopping until she had his cock cupped in her palm.

"Especially there," he said as he thrust deeper into her hand.

"Then maybe you should take your jeans off."

"Maybe I should. And maybe I can take your pajamas off while I'm at it," he suggested.

"I think that's a great idea." She nibbled on her bottom lip, bringing her hands to the buttons of her top, slipping them off one by one. He had yet to move, so she knew he was watching. Her heart raced a little faster. She loved her body. It wasn't perfect, but she had generous curves, that she hoped he would appreciate. Baring herself to him fueled her fire, dampening her folds.

"Jesus, fuck, Maddison. You're stunning." One finger traced from her neck down to her breast, leaving a trail of fire on her skin where he touched. He paused at her nipple, circling around it once, twice, then moving on to the next. "Absolutely perfect."

He moved so fast, she only had a moment's notice of his hot breath on her breast before he had the stiff peak in his mouth, sucking with gentle but insistent pressure. She moaned as she ran her fingers through his hair, holding him to her. His hands moved to push the fabric off her shoulders, then went to her hips, tugging at the bottoms to get them down. She lifted off the bed, helping him along.

When she was completely nude, yet still mostly covered by the blankets, she tightened her fists in his hair. "Now it's your turn," she said.

He pulled his mouth from her nipple with a pop, then came up to kiss her lips again. "I could feast on your body for hours and not tire of it."

Her clit throbbed at the thought of his mouth down there but now wasn't the time. She needed him, all of him. Another time, they could go slow. "Later. Please, take your jeans off."

He wiggled next to her, shifting his weight this way, and that, before finally coming back to her. When he pushed her so that her back was against the mattress, he followed, pressing his chest against her breasts, and her hips cradled him. He was so close to where she needed him most, but he made no move to penetrate. Instead, his lips found hers again, and his hands roamed her body, in a slow, torturous, exhilarating caress. He shifted his weight so that he could explore lower, and her whole body tensed. She wanted him to touch her everywhere, but especially there.

He slid his hand down one inner thigh and back up again, then down the other. As he was about to go higher again, she ground up against him. "Please, touch me, Luke." She wasn't afraid of asking for what she wanted, and she wanted more.

"Tell me what you want, Maddison. Do you want me to suck on those gorgeous nipples of yours again?"

A bolt of pleasure streaked down her body to land in her clit.

"Or do you want me to slide my fingers into your pussy?" he asked before she could answer.

"Yes, both, please." She gasped as his lips locked around her nipple again. They'd only started, but she was already close to orgasm.

He moaned, sending the vibration from his mouth to her breast, and she thought she might come from that alone. He slid his hand between her thighs, cupped her, the heat from his palm making her throb even more. "Tell me, Maddie. Hearing your voice while I touch you is making me so hard I can't think straight."

She didn't hesitate. "Touch me. I want your fingers on my clit, and in my pussy. And your cock..."

When his fingers slid between her folds, she couldn't continue. The intense pleasure rushing through her took the breath from her lungs. She couldn't think. He slid the pads of his fingers around and around her clit, building the pressure within to new heights. Just as she was about to fall over the edge, his fingers were gone, and she whimpered at the loss. "Please," she begged.

He grazed his teeth along the soft flesh of her breast. His teeth, pointier than they had been, only made her want to press harder into his mouth.

"I want to be inside you when I make you come for the first time, Maddison. I want to feel each tremor, and every single tightening muscle around my cock while you shatter in my arms." He took her nipple into his mouth again, sucking hard. When he finally positioned himself between her thighs, she thought the sensual torture was over, but his thrusts only had him stroking between her folds with his shaft. The throbbing in her clit intensified, but it wasn't enough. She needed him inside her like she'd never needed a man before.

Just because he was happy taking his time didn't mean she had to make it easy for him. Maddie drove her fingers through his hair, tugging until he came up to kiss her lips. She kept him there, thrusting her tongue into his mouth, savoring him as he'd done her. When she broke free, she kissed along his jaw and down his neck. She slid her hands over the hard ridges of his chest, stopping only once she reached the little loops in both nipples. She gave them a little flick, then a small tug. Luke moaned, and tilted his hips against hers again—harder.

"I want you to fuck me, Luke. I need you inside me, now," she whispered into his ear. His arms tightened around her and a soft growl rumbled from his chest. The sound was way too sexy to be anything but the dragon's reaction to what she'd said. She continued kissing down his neck, then when she reached his shoulder, she nipped at his skin. Not hard, but enough that he felt it.

Luke's body tightened and he remained still for a second, but in the next beat, he lifted himself from her body, positioned himself, and finally slid into her.

He filled her, stretching her until there was no room for anything but him.

"Maddie," came his hoarse whisper, "are you okay? Did I hurt you?"

She shook her head, and loving the reaction she had received from her first bite, she did it again.

"Fuck, Maddie," he moaned before he started retreating from her body.

For a moment she thought she might have done something wrong, but as he was about to leave her entirely, he thrust back in again. As though sensing the pleasure rushing through her had culminated on her clit, he reached between them, stroking her with one long finger. He continued the slow, deliberate pace until her body had adjusted to his girth—until she couldn't stand the pressure building inside.

On the next inward thrust, Maddie met him halfway, making them both moan. She was sending him a signal, one that he heard loud and clear. Each stroke came harder, and faster, until her whole body quivered. Luke kissed his way to the base of her neck, and she tilted head, giving him more room. She loved having her neck kissed. His lips, his finger and his cock all worked together, building her pleasure until she couldn't keep from crying out. His teeth scraped at the base of her neck, then just as deep spasms rocked her body, he bit her.

« CHAPTER 8 »

Maddie lay motionless beneath him. Luke still felt the milder aftershocks of her orgasm squeezing him, but she didn't utter a sound. Didn't budge. He had been so caught up in what he was doing, and how damned good it felt, that when she had bared her neck to him, he hadn't stopped himself from biting her. It wasn't a mate's mark, but it didn't get any closer.

"Maddie…" He had no idea what he had been about to say, but he had to say something.

After a moment, she brought her hands to his cheeks and kissed his lips. "I've never experienced anything like that before."

"Are you okay?"

She got an odd look on her face, her brows drawn down a little. "Of course I am. But we're not done here." She nipped at his chin, then tilted her pelvis, sheathing him inside her again.

"I didn't hurt you? When I bit you?" It had to have hurt. The dragon's bite was much stronger than a human's.

"No. My turn." She pushed against his shoulder indicating that she wanted him to move. The moment he turned onto his side, then his back, she followed, straddling him. She didn't wait for him to take the lead, reaching down between them, she positioned herself over him and sank down until he was all the way in again. Maddie threw her head back and moaned, giving him a gorgeous view of her breasts. He was about to come up to suckle them again, when she placed her hands on his chest, stopping him.

"Not this time," she said. "I'm playing now." Her fingers traced the muscles of his abdomen, then his chest and shoulders, all the while, she rocked on top of him. He expected her to go back to his nipple rings, was eager for it, but she kept her hands away from them. She moved faster, lifting her hips a little more with each grinding thrust. His cock throbbed with each moan that slipped past her lips as she ground her clit against him.

He brought his hands to her hips, lifting her higher, then helping her come back down onto him faster.

"Did you bite me, or was it the dragon?" she asked, her voice low, and silky.

He didn't want to admit it, but he wouldn't lie. "Maybe a bit of both."

He lifted her again, and she whimpered as he slid her back down, grinding his pelvis into her clit. She leaned forward, coming to within a couple of inches of his mouth. "So if I bit your neck, would your dragon like that?"

He slid her up and down again, and the muscles inside her gripped him hard. "Hell, yes."

She gave him a little grin, then brought her mouth down to his neck, her hand to his left nipple, then tugged on the ring, before clamping down on his neck—hard.

Luke couldn't hold back. With a muffled roar, he thrust up into her, as he brought her down over and over again until their mingled cries filled the room. Maddie's pussy clenched and released around him, milking him. When she finally released his neck and her orgasm overtook her, she brought him right along with her.

Maddie collapsed against him, and he wrapped his arms around her. What in the hell had he ever done to deserve such a woman?

It took a few minutes for his heart to stop racing, and by then, he could feel the goosebumps prickling at her skin. "What do you say we either get you back under the covers or get you dressed? You're freezing."

Maddie smiled against his chest. "I'm starving. How about we grab a shower, then we can go find a place with some heat and have breakfast?"

"Now that would be wonderful, except that I doubt you have any hot water," he laughed.

"Oh, right."

"I'll tell you what? I'll warm up enough water for you to freshen up, and then we'll go eat. Maybe by the time we get back, the power will be on and we can enjoy the shower." He couldn't use his fire without shifting, and there was no way he could do that inside, but if he had a basin of water, he could use his body heat to warm it so that it wasn't ice cold.

"Okay," she scooted to the aside and let him up. "I'll wait in here while you do that." She grabbed the blankets and pulled them all the way up to her chin, cutting off his view of her luscious body. Not that it mattered. He'd have plenty of opportunities to see it over the course of their long lives.

He leaned in and gave her a kiss on her cold nose. "I'll be right back."

Luke didn't bother dressing, going to the kitchen to get a pot was a short walk, and once he amped up his body heat, he'd be plenty warm. He carried the pot to the bathroom, filled it, then placed both hands inside. It took five, minutes to warm the water until she could wash without freezing, but he waited until it would be nice and warm for her before calling her in.

"That was fast," she said as she walked into the room as naked as he was.

Luke groaned.

"What's wrong?" She nibbled at her bottom lip, and he wanted to groan a second time.

"I have to get out of here. Otherwise, I'm going to drag you back to bed, and you won't get to eat anything today at all." He gave her a long, lingering kiss before he slipped past her to go find his clothes.

Josephine's Diner wasn't far, and like Maddie's house, it didn't have power, but they had set up a generator out back and the place was warm-ish. If he sat next to Maddie, he could keep her warm enough.

He led Maddie to the only empty booth left in the place, let her scoot onto the bench, and then slid in next to her. He grabbed the beat up tri-fold that passed for a menu and started reading. "What are you in the mood for," he asked.

"Oh, I don't know—"

"Don't bother looking at the menu," an older waitress with bleach blond hair and a raspy smoker's voice said as she approached the table with her coffee pot in hand. "We don't have a lot of power. We're serving omelets, no toast, and nothing else. Do you want coffee?"

"Please," he responded. "Maddie?"

"No, thank you. Can I have a glass of orange juice instead, and an omelet sounds wonderful. Thanks."

"Same here," he smiled at the woman who gave him an annoyed stare in response. He didn't bother asking what kind of omelets they were serving for fear of irritating the woman further.

"Actually, can you double up his omelet? If that's all we're having, I'm sure a regular one won't be quite enough," Maddie asked, her cheeks turning a bright pink. "Thanks."

A warm fuzzy feeling filled him. Already his mate was looking out for him. Of course, a regular omelet wouldn't be anywhere near enough to fill his dragon-sized appetite, but he hadn't wanted to make special requests of the already put-upon woman.

"It'll cost double. I don't make exceptions for *his* kind." The venomous words caught him a little off-guard, but he wouldn't let them rile him. There were idiots in all parts of the world, and Glen Farley was no exception.

He'd assumed the woman had been grumpy because she was busy, but no, she just didn't like dragons. The woman looked at him, then Maddie, and then grunted when she saw the pink spot where he'd bitten her peeking past the collar of her shirt.

"That's fine," he told her, not wanting the irritating woman to say something to upset Maddie. All he wanted to do was get some food into his mate so they could leave. The looks some of the men were giving him had his stomach churning. He could take them all, no problem, but he had Maddie to worry about now. If she got hurt, even accidentally, he didn't know if he'd be able to control the dragon. If feeling his scales close to the surface had frightened her, experiencing a full dragon's rage would send her running for the hills.

Once the waitress was gone, he turned his attention back to his mate, refusing to allow the other patrons to ruin his time with her. He'd deal with whatever came along, and keep her safe, too. He draped an arm around her shoulder and tucked her in close, sharing his warmth with her. "So, what are your plans for Christmas?"

"I'm staying home. I might stop in to see Marybeth, Gloria, and the kids, but that's about it." She smiled at him, but her voice was more than a little sad.

"You don't have any family in the area?"

"No, my mom is back home. My dad died before I was born. I moved here a few months ago, so I don't really know all that many people. I'm lucky I ran into Gloria at the store one day, and she took me under her wing."

"I'd understand if you said no, but I'd love for you to spend it up at the estate with me." He didn't have to ask the others to know that they'd be happy to have her. In fact, Stella would be thrilled to have another woman to talk to. As well as they all got along, he could only imagine that she must miss female companionship.

"I couldn't impose. That's only two days away. There's no time to prepare for an extra person in that time."

"It's no imposition, we have plenty of food, and I have three bedrooms in my section of the house alone. There's more than enough room." Luke looked up when he heard the chime of the door, then his heart sank. "Crap. I'm in trouble."

"What?" Her hand came up to rest on his forearm. "What's the matter?"

Luke laughed. "Nothing serious. I was supposed to call Stella when I got to your place last night. When you opened the door with your head banged up, I totally forgot. My reminder just walked into the Diner."

***

"Yeah, I found him. He's safe, but not for long." A deep, male voice broke in. The sound of someone removing their coat, and then sliding on the bench across from her had her eyebrows lifting. She let go of his arm and slid her hand down to his thigh. "I'll be home soon," the man paused for a second, then "I love you too, baby."

"Forgetting something," the man said after another moment.

"Dude, I'm sorry. I totally forgot to call. In my defense, I had other things on my mind when I got here."

The man's deep, throaty laugh helped her relax a little. "I'm sure you did, but I meant you hadn't introduced me to this pretty woman snuggled up next to you."

She felt Luke's chuckle against her side. "Sorry, Brycen, this is Maddison, my mate. Maddie, this is Brycen. He's Stella's mate. She probably drove him crazy all night, and again this morning worrying because I hadn't reported in."

"Nice to meet you, Brycen," she extended her hand across the table. His hand when he took hers was as warm as Luke's. Another dragon.

"It's a pleasure to meet you, too, Maddie. There's another storm front coming in, Luke. I'm heading back up the mountain. I suggest that if you plan on coming home today that you do so earlier rather than later," he told him.

"I will. Tell Stella that I'm sorry. I didn't mean to worry her." The sincerity in Luke's voice made her smile. He really did care a lot about his family.

"I'm going to the bakery for some of those cookies before I head back. Need anything?"

"Hey, why don't you let us get the cookies. It can be a peace offering when I get back. I'm trying to convince Maddie to come up to the estate for the holidays," Luke told Brycen.

"You really should, Maddie," Brycen added. "Stella would love it. We all would."

She heard the heeled footsteps before the waitress reached the table, and cringed. A plate was dropped in front of her, then another in front of Luke.

"We're out of eggs," the snarly woman said. "Do you want some coffee?" she presumably asked Brycen.

"No, I'm good. I was just leaving."

"Even better," she said, and then plodded off to another table.

"What the hell was that about?" he asked.

"Dragon hater. Don't worry. As soon as we eat our breakfast we're heading out of here," Luke assured. A long heavy silence followed.

"You know what? I think I could use a coffee. In fact, yours looks damned good. Enjoy your orange juice," Brycen said.

Maddie heard the slide of a cup across the table.

"It's not great coffee anyway," Luke said, his voice a little lighter than it had been.

"Okay, what's going on?" She faced Luke. "I can't see, so you have to tell me if something is wrong."

"Some of the customers aren't looking too friendly, that's all," he told her. "It's nothing we can't handle."

She nodded. "Does this happen to you guys a lot?"

"No, not anymore. Once upon a time, it was common, but people are more accepting these days, for the most part," Brycen added. "Some still don't like to see us interacting with humans, though."

Are you serious? They're upset because Luke and I are together?" As odd as it was to say that about someone she'd just met, it felt right.

"It's not worth worrying about," Luke said and kissed her temple. "We'll eat, grab some cookies—oh wait, if there isn't any power, they can't bake."

"That's right. Maybe we can grab some things and Stella and I can bake some instead?" Maddie offered.

"You mean it? You'll come up to the estate for the holidays?" Luke asked, his voice lifting a little.

She smiled in his direction and nodded. "Yeah, I'd love to spend the holidays with you if you don't think anyone else will mind."

"They won't."

"No, they won't, not one bit," Brycen added.

"Great, let's eat so we can get out of here before the snow begins to fall again. We'll stop by your place and grab what you'll need, then take the truck up. It's too cold for me to fly you up there."

Fly her up there? She hadn't even considered the possibility. "You could do that?" she asked, a little thrill of excitement rushing through her.

"Well, yeah, if you wanted me to. You'd have to hold on, but it's safe," he said almost absently. "Does this smell right to you?"

Did what smell right? She opened her mouth to ask, but Brycen spoke first. "No, it doesn't. Don't eat it." His voice was much sharper and colder than it had been only moments before.

"Come on, we'll eat at the estate," Luke said as he stood.

She didn't know what was going on, but both men were pissed. She hadn't smelled a thing, but if they could smell something wrong with the eggs, then she wasn't about to argue.

"Problem with the eggs?" The cranky waitress said as she came over.

"Yeah, there is. We're not paying for them so you can forget about that. I'll pay for the coffee and the juice," Luke told her.

"Now you listen here, you ordered the food, and you're going to pay for it."

"Is there a problem here, Josie?" Another man's voice came into the conversation.

"No problem," Brycen added, and she felt his heat on the other side of her. "Something was added to the omelets to make my friends sick. Luckily, our noses are more sensitive than yours are. I'd suggest you all be careful with your meals," he said loud enough for the other patrons to hear.

"You bastard. Get the hell out of my restaurant." Josie hissed. "There's nothing wrong with the food here."

"Fine. I'll give you fifty bucks if you take a bite of this omelet."

Maddie heard a scrape, and could only imagine that Brycen had grabbed one of the plates from the table to offer the woman.

"You're out of your mind if you think I'd eat anything a dragon had its paws on," the woman spat.

"I didn't think so. Let's get out of here."

"Here's your coat, Maddie," Luke said as he helped her into it.

The entire place was silent, and no one bothered them as they made their way to the door.

"Don't bother coming back here again," Josie yelled at them as they walked out.

« CHAPTER 9 »

The churning in Luke's gut intensified as they walked back toward Maddie's apartment. Thankfully it was only a few blocks.

"I'm sticking around until you guys get in the truck, then I'll grab what you'll need for the cookies before heading back up," Brycen said.

"Thanks," he took Maddie's hand in his. He didn't want to alarm her, but the sooner they got out of Glen Farley, the better as far as he was concerned. He quickened his step a little, and she followed suit. It was probably nothing. They hadn't seen or sensed any hunters since Brycen and Stella were mated, but that didn't mean they weren't around. It just meant they hadn't been close enough to be detected. He knew something was wrong the moment they opened the front door to the apartment building. The entire lobby reeked of foul human stench. It wasn't that all humans smelled bad. Maddie was proof that some smelled damned amazing, but it was the adrenaline combined with the fear when humans were up to no good that stunk so bad.

"Do you smell that?" Luke asked for the second time that day.

"Yep," Brycen answered. "How about if you take Maddie home, and I'll see what's what?"

"Wait, I need my things," Maddie said. "Whatever you're smelling, surely I can run in and grab a few things. I'll make it quick."

"How about if we let Brycen take a look around, and as long as it's safe to go in, we will." He didn't want to freak her out, but her safety came first, even before her sense of independence.

"Okay," she agreed. "Be careful. Here's my key." She fished it out of her pocket and held it for him to take. "I'm on the second floor, third door on the left, apartment C."

The moment he opened the door to the stairwell, the stench intensified. Whoever was there, or had been there, had used the stairs. Luke gave Brycen a pointed look. His jaw ached as fury roiled inside him, and his teeth poked at his gums, threatening to push through.

It took Brycen less than a minute to get to her apartment. His mighty roar shook the walls, letting Luke know that whatever he'd found, wasn't good. Maddie gasped and clung tighter to his hand. Luke wanted to rush up there, but there was no way he was leaving Maddie unprotected.

"We should go up there and help him," she said, her voice high pitched and tight.

"He's okay. If he were in battle, I'd hear it," he assured her. He didn't mention that most of Glen Farley would hear it if that were the case.

The door to the stairwell slammed open again. "It's safe to go up. There's no one in the apartment, but I have to tell you, Maddie, someone was there. The place was trashed," Brycen said, his words clipped.

She released Luke's hand, covering her mouth with her own. "Why would someone do that? I have nothing of value in there."

"I don't know, love. But we'll figure it out." Luke grabbed his cell and dialed 911. Might as well get this sorted out, then they could go. She wouldn't be allowed to take any of her things until the police had come and gone, anyway.

Brycen stepped off to the side, but didn't go far, and made a call to Stella, letting her know that they'd be later than expected. It didn't take long that two uniformed officers came in. Brycen told him what he'd seen, and assured them that he hadn't touched anything before they went up to investigate.

"You're free to go up now. Be careful, there's broken glass and debris on the floor," the officers warned when they finally came down again. "I'd like to remind you, gentlemen, that we will take care of the investigation, and everything to do with this case."

Luke could only nod, fury making it impossible for him to utter a word.

"Of course, officer," Brycen replied.

Maddie, who had been quiet since the officers had arrived, trembled when Luke took her into his arms. He shoved the dragon back with all his might, forcing his jaw to work. She wasn't in danger, but she needed him, and flying into a rage wouldn't help soothe her. "Let's get your things."

He let her lead the way, even though he wanted to keep her right next to him, or even behind him so he could shield her, but he wouldn't take away her power.

When they reached the second floor, the dragon surged forward again. His scales came as close to the surface as they could come without breaking through. On the wall leading to her apartment, someone had spray painted in large red letters, "dragon whore", and "dragon fucker".

Her door was busted open, and hanging on one hinge. Inside her furniture was streaked with the same red paint. Someone had taken a knife to her couch cushions, and her things were thrown everywhere.

His growl burst free, low, and mean, but he couldn't keep it in. Whoever had done it, hadn't left anything intact. Nothing of hers was salvageable.

"Luke, tell me," she pleaded.

"He can't talk right now, Maddie," Brycen stepped in. "I can take you to your room while Luke gets his thoughts together, but I don't think anything can be saved. I'm sorry."

Her distressed whimper snapped him out of the rage gripping him. In an instant, he took her in his arms. He took long deep breaths as she cried against his chest, struggling to regain his control. By the time she stopped sniffling, he was ready to help her deal with whatever she needed.

"Tell me what you need, and I'll see if we can bring it," he offered. "You won't be able to walk around without getting hurt."

"I don't want anything. Let's go. Maybe we can stop at the store before heading out? I'll need a change of clothes, and a toothbrush." She shuddered against him, then pulled back, straightening her spine. "Oh, I need my walking cane. I keep it by the door. I didn't grab it when we left earlier because you were with me."

Luke looked at Brycen, who snapped his teeth together and shook his head.

"I'm sorry, baby, we'll get you a new one," he said.

She made a strangled sound but then lifted her chin again. "I have to order it online. They don't sell anything like that here. I'll be fine. I'll have to be careful and do a lot of counting once we get to your house, but I'll be okay."

"That's right. And there's plenty of us around to help you when you need it."

"How many people live there?" she asked.

"Eleven, counting Stella, but at any given time, half the men are on assignment. Most of them will be home for Christmas though." He hoped she didn't mind the chaos of the household when everyone was around.

"And poor Stella has to take care of all of you?" she said, her eyebrows lifting high as they walked across the lobby toward the front door again.

"See, already she knows how you guys use and abuse me," Stella said as she came off the wall she'd been leaning against.

"Hey, what are you doing here?" Brycen asked as he went to his mate and gave her a big kiss on the lips.

As always, seeing the two of them together made him smile. "Stella, this is Maddie. Maddie, Stella," Luke introduced them once Brycen released her.

"I'm so glad to meet you. When Luke told us he'd found you, we were all very excited," Stella said. "I decided to come into the village to meet you since Brycen was being so mysterious when he called."

Luke breathed a sigh of relief when she didn't bring up the break in. Brycen had told her about it on the phone. He'd whispered, so he didn't think Maddie had heard, but Luke hadn't missed a word. It was just like Stella to come rushing over to make sure they were alright.

"Stella, we have to go do some shopping, and then we're going to head home. Maddie has agreed to stay with us for the holidays."

"Are you freaking kidding me?" Stella shouted with a high pitched squeal. "That's fantastic. I haven't been shopping with a girl in forever, and I'm not going to be the only girl around the house for a change." She came over and linked her arm around Maddie's and led her to the front door. "This is going to be so much fun."

Luke grinned at Brycen, loving Stella a little bit more for the warm welcome she'd given his mate. Not that he'd expected anything less from her, but it made his heart swell just the same.

« CHAPTER 10 »

Maddie stood at the register, another protest teetering at the tip of her tongue. They had already gone through the first of two department stores in Glen Farley and purchased way more clothes and other things they all thought she needed than she could afford in a year, and here they were in the other, ringing up yet another ridiculously large order. While the two women shopped for clothing, the men had gone off, claiming to save time by getting the baking supplies they needed for the cookies, but she knew they wanted to discuss the break-in at her place.

"Oh, wait," Stella said. "We need to get you something sexy to sleep in."

Maddie's cheeks burned. "That's not necessary. This is so much more than I should be getting already."

"Nonsense. Luke will love it," Stella protested.

"Really, I can't afford this. Even if I don't spend a penny on anything else for the next three years, I won't be able to pay for this," she whispered. She hated admitting it to her new friend, but she had to say something.

Stella laughed and took her by the hand. "Are you kidding me? Our men have more money than any of us could spend in our lifetimes, and dragons do live long. Come on, just a couple more things."

Maddie took a deep breath, and caught a whiff of Luke nearby, but she let Stella drag her off again. By the time they were all done, the men had to make two trips back and forth from their carts to the truck that Brycen had so kindly flown to get after they'd left her place.

Each time Stella and Brycen were close, she heard the smooches and Stella's giggles. It was obvious she adored her mate, and he her as well. The first snowflakes came down as they said goodbye to Brycen, and Stella, who chose to fly home rather than ride. She thanked them both for their help, and then they were gone. Luke didn't talk much on the way up the mountain. He drove slowly, and she had to wonder how bad the roads were, but she wasn't afraid. He'd keep her safe. When he'd lost control in her apartment, and he'd held her, his scales had been just under his skin. She could feel them where her cheek had rested on his chest, and where she'd snuck her fingers under his open jacket, but he'd been so gentle, so tender. The beast inside him did not define the man.

"Thank you for today, Luke. I don't know what I would have done without you," she said.

He reached over and linked his fingers through hers, bringing them up to his lips for a kiss. "Spoiling you will be my new life's mission," he told her.

"I think you've done enough. Seriously, thank you."

"You're welcome."

The truck slid a little to the side, proving that the roads were as slick as she'd imagined. "Is it much farther?"

"Nope, we'll be turning off onto our private property here in a sec." He let go of her hand as he slowed the vehicle and the click of the turn signal sounded.

It had taken less than an hour to get there, even with the weather. After a few minutes, he pulled the truck to a stop, waited a few seconds, then drove a short distance. She waited for him to round the truck to help her climb back down. Her feet landed on cement, and the mechanical smells of a garage greeted her.

"There you guys are. I thought we'd have to send a search party," Stella said when Luke led her inside.

"Can you show her around the main living quarters? I'm sure there are some things that Maddie will need to know so she can familiarize herself—"

"Yeah, yeah, don't worry, we'll be fine," Stella said as she took her hand and led her away. "So from the garage, you turn right to go into the main living area. To the right are the living quarters of some of the men, but you won't need to go in there too much. Luke lives in the other wing. That's where Brycen and I are, as well as some of the others. It's a huge place, but you'll get used to it."

Maddie took a few steps when Luke's hand came to rest on her shoulder. He cleared his throat before speaking. "I have three bedrooms in my part of the house. Two spare rooms, and my bedroom. I know where I want you to stay, but it's your choice, love. Where should I bring your new things?"

Her cheeks heated. Stella was still right next to her, but it didn't matter. She didn't want to be anywhere else. "If it's okay, I'd like to stay with you," she said.

"It's more than okay. Have fun. I'll come looking for you once I get the stuff out of the truck and upstairs." He gave her a quick kiss on the lips, and she smiled.

"Okay." She imagined she must look pretty goofy, but she didn't care. If all the smooching she heard going on in the stores were anything to go by, the others in the house would be used to seeing it.

« CHAPTER 11 »

Luke gave Stella as much time as he could tolerate with Maddie before he went looking for her. He'd gone in search of his clan mates and told them of what had happened. Of course, Brycen had already informed them, and a plan was being put in place to seek out the bastards who had trashed her house. Next, he sought out his clansmen who were handy with tools, and put together a team to go to her apartment to start fixing the place up again. He hoped she'd stay with him, but if she wanted to go back there, he didn't want her to have to deal with any of it.

He looked at his watch, certain it had been hours since he's seen her, and was surprised to see it hadn't even been one. He found the women in the kitchen. Maddie had her hands buried in a large bowl that smelled of something sweet with nutmeg. His stomach growled, reminding him that it was time to get some real food into his woman. The fast food burger and fries they'd eaten between department stores was long gone, at least, it was for him.

"Smells delicious already. I can't wait until you get those in the oven." The way her smile widened when she heard his voice had his heart beating a little faster, and his own smile splitting his face. He went over to her, wrapped his arms around her waist and pressed a kiss to her neck. He'd love nothing more than to steal her away and spend some time alone with her in his quarters, but he wouldn't be selfish. The joy shining on her face more than made up for the time he had to share her with Stella. "Do you want a bite to eat? I'm famished."

"I could eat," she said as she leaned into him.

"I'll let you get finished with what you're doing while I get some food ready. Maybe if I cook something edible you'll let me have some cookies for dessert?"

Stella excused herself, he was sure to give them some space, as well as go find Brycen. Once she was out of the room, he brought his hands down to her hips and pulled her closer. She gasped before shifting her ass against his growing cock. He stifled his moan in her neck, kissing her again.

"I think that sounds wonderful," She said, her voice soft and sexy.

"Which, the food, or me," he asked.

"Both, but mostly you," she giggled and rubbed her ass against him again.

"Break it up, you two." Jace said as he walked into the kitchen and headed to the fridge for a bottle of beer, but then did a double-take when he spotted them. "Oh, hey, sorry. I'm so used to hearing those kinds of giggles from Stella that I thought it was her and Brycen in here."

Maddie stiffened, and would have pulled away had it not been for the fact that he pinned her against the counter. "Jace, this is Maddie. Maddie, meet Jace, Stella's brother."

He came over to where they stood, and peered into the mixing bowl her hands were still buried in. "Can't wait to try those," he said. "Stella tells me you're staying over Christmas. I'm happy to hear it. We're going to cut a tree tomorrow, maybe you'd like to come along?"

Maddie was nodding even before Jace finished his sentence. "That would be lovely. I've never done that before."

Luke wrapped his arms around her waist, and she relaxed into him. Every one of his clan mates went out of their way to make her feel welcomed. "We're using sleds to do it, so you'll have to borrow one of Stella's snow suits. I'm sure she has extras, unless of course she thought to pick one up for you today."

Maddie laughed. "To be honest, we bought so much, I can't even remember what I have, but if the number of bags we brought back here are any indication, there must be one in there somewhere."

"Great. We'll look through them and get your clothes settled into the closet after we eat." He kissed her neck again, noticing—and ignoring—the exaggerated eye roll Jace gave them. Luke grabbed the chicken from the fridge and got what he needed before getting to work a little ways down from Maddie. He wasn't a great chef, but he could toss chicken in some spiced bread crumbs like a pro. Before he even had all the ingredients out, Stella came back, her cheeks flushed, and a small smile on her lips. He didn't even want to know.

"Oh, you making more food? I think Brycen will want to eat again, if you don't mind putting a few more pieces in, I'd appreciate it. I made some potato salad earlier, and I'm sure there's enough for the two of you if you want some to go with the chicken."

"Sure thing," he said. He'd already planned on cooking extra. If the other couple didn't have it, one of the other men would when they came in later.

Once he had it in the oven, he gave Maddison a hug and a kiss before excusing himself. She didn't need him hovering over her like a mother hen. Stella would take care of her. With that in mind, he headed for the front of the house. He had roughly twenty-five minutes before he had to take the meat out of the oven, which gave him plenty of time to stretch his wings a little.

***

Maddie didn't remember the last time she'd had such a good time. Stella was funny as all hell, and kept the conversation going as though they'd known each other for years. Every once in a while she'd hear someone coming into the front part of the house, or some muted voiced, but otherwise, no one came in to bother them as they laughed and rolled out the cookies.

When the chicken was almost ready, Luke came back, his hair was a little damp when she hugged him, and he had a fresh outdoorsy scent about him. Even though Stella had walked her through the entire main area of the house and shown her where the dining room was, they took their plates to the kitchen table where the other couple joined them. When it was finally done, and all the cookies were out of the oven, Maddie was dead tired. The entire day had been like something out of a dream. If she pushed the memory of the Diner and her apartment aside, it had been the best day she'd had in a very long time.

The four of them worked together to square away the kitchen, then Brycen and Stella excused themselves for the evening. As intimate as they had been the previous night, and all they had gone through together that day, she shouldn't be shy around Luke, but, doubt started creeping in.

"You sure you want me staying in your room? I could take a guest room if you want."

Luke laughed, and she felt silly for asking. "Are you kidding me?" he asked. "There's nowhere else I'd rather have you than right there with me. I want to go to sleep with you in my arms, and wake up wrapped around you every morning like I did this morning."

The following day, all geared up in her brand new snowsuit, and a helmet she borrowed from Stella, she accompanied everyone to get a Christmas tree. At first, she'd clung to Luke for dear life as the snow machine roared to life, but by the time they found the perfect tree, the exhilaration of the ride had made her almost giddy. Even the cold didn't bother her when she was snuggled up against him. They followed it up with steaming cups of hot chocolate and the cookies she and Stella had made the day before.

As much fun as the day had been, the night was even better. Luke took his time, discovering every inch of her body, and she explored him with her fingers and mouth, learning each defined muscle, and plane. His lovemaking, sweet, and sensual one moment, turned wild and passionate the next.

Christmas Eve, Luke woke her with the smell of bacon, eggs, and coffee. They snuggled in bed for a while, talking a little, and kissing a lot. She could get used to the attention. When he left her to shower, she couldn't wipe the smile off her face. Being with Luke was like being home. Talking with him, laughing, just being together was... right. There was no other way to explain it. She had never had that kind of connection with anyone, and doubted she ever would again. More than that, she didn't want it with anyone else. For someone who needed months to begin to trust people, she couldn't imagine not having him there anymore. Luke had told her that some of his clan mates were already cleaning up and fixing her place, but did she really want to go back there? Without him?

With the master bathroom attached to the bedroom, she hadn't bothered to bring in her clothes, so when she came out with nothing but a towel wrapped around her, she wasn't surprised to hear Luke's sexy growl.

"So gorgeous. It's amazing I can walk upright at all with you around," he said as he came to her and wrapped her in his arms. He brought his hands to her bottom, pulling her in tight, proving how much her partial nudity affected him. She was so tempted to take advantage of their time together, but she had to get ready.

She and Stella were going back to the village. They had made more goodies, and were delivering them to Marybeth and Gloria. Apparently the truck was loaded with gifts for all the foster children, too. She couldn't wait to hear their squeals of laughter, and have their little arms around her. Gloria had told her of the horrors some of those children had gone through. It amazed her that they still laughed, and played, happy to be in a safe home for the first time in their short lives.

"As much as I want to take you up on what your body is offering," she gave him a long lingering kiss, "and I do want to, I have to go."

"What? You mean I can't keep you holed up here in my bedroom forever? I promise I'd make it worth your while," he teased.

"I'm sure you would." She kissed him again but then pulled away. "I'll tell you what. Once I get back, I'll be all yours for the rest of the day." She went to the closet and picked an outfit. She and Stella had gone through each one they had bought and had organized them in sets so she would match and not have to keep asking for help to choose her clothing.

"Deal," he said when she returned to the room to get dressed. "But before you go, I have a present for you."

"It's not even Christmas yet. Why are you giving me a present?"

"This is more necessity than something fun and frivolous, so it's not a Christmas present, just a gift. I didn't know what to get, so I got a few. Try them out, and if you don't like any of them, we'll return them all and get something else."

"I'm sure whatever you got me will be wonderful." One of the reasons she was so happy to be going into the village was so that she could find a little gift for Luke for Christmas morning. She didn't have a whole lot of money, but she could buy him something. She just didn't know what.

"Here, sit on the bed. I'll get them for you." He walked over to the dresser and came back. "Hold out your hand." When she did, he placed a handle on her outstretched palm.

"A walking stick?" She gripped the handle, and stroked its length with her other hand. "Luke, that's so thoughtful. Thank you. How did you get it here so fast?"

"I had them put a rush on it, and when they wouldn't deliver to Glen Farley, I had Matt fly to Denver to get it. Try it out. I have three more here. I had them customized to your height already."

Once she had tried all four, she chose one, but to be honest, they all felt like a perfect fit. "Thank you so much. They're all wonderful. Any of them will do."

"Great, so we'll keep them all," he announced. "If you need more, let me know, the company will keep your information on file. Now when you're in the village, you'll be able to walk safely without having to be dragged around. And here too, I guess. Once you're used to the layout of the house, you'll be able to go wherever you want."

She didn't know what to say. Luke, with his thoughtfulness, had given her her freedom back, limited as it was for a person without sight. She kissed him, with all she had, showing him how much his gift meant to her. When he finally pulled away, she was the one to protest, making him laugh. "You're going to miss your ride if you don't go."

Had it not been for Stella waiting for her, she would have gladly stayed right where she was for the rest of the day. "I know. But when I get back, you're all mine," she promised.

"I'm counting on it," he said, his voice so gravelly it sent a shiver through her at the memory of their lovemaking when his dragon rose to play. "Be careful down there. If anyone bothers you or Stella, I want you to come straight home."

"We'll be careful." She gave him one more quick kiss before going to the door, more confident now that she had the cane to guide her.

« CHAPTER 12 »

Their first stop was the Woolridge house. The instant they walked in the door, they were bombarded with hugs and kisses. Even little Andrew, the newest addition to the foster family, came for a tentative hug. The women worked magic with the children, drawing them out of the shells they were in when they arrived, turning them back into the children they should have been to begin with.

They spent the next couple of hours handing out gifts and munching on cookies. The kids laughed and played all around them. As much as she enjoyed it, when Stella suggested they get going, she was happy to go. She needed to do a bit of shopping, and wanted to get back to Luke, so the sooner they got going, the sooner they'd be home.

After what felt like hours of shopping, Maddie groaned and hung her head. "I don't know what to get him. I have no idea what he'd like, and even if I did, he has everything he could possibly want, or need."

"Can I be honest with you, Maddie?" Stella asked.

"Please. I'm all out of ideas."

"There is only one thing that he wants. That's you. You don't have to buy him a thing. Let's get him a nice sweater so he'll have a gift under the tree, and we'll see what we can figure out for your *real* gift."

"But he already has me."

"Not completely. Maybe we need to have a girl to girl talk so you know what to expect, and then you can figure out what you want to do."

They stopped at a small coffee shop, and by the time they were done, her mind was whirling. What she was planning was insane—beyond insane—but excitement rushed through her at the prospect. They made one last stop at the lingerie shop before heading back.

As soon as the truck came to a stop, the door was ripped open, and Luke was there, helping her out. He didn't say a word, but Maddie knew something was wrong. His touch wasn't cold or impersonal, but he was coiled so tight, she thought he might snap. "What's the matter?"

He didn't say a word, as he wrapped her in his arms, and held her—tight.

"No problems in the village?" This time, it was Brycen's voice she heard, and he sounded as anxious as Luke did.

"No, not at all," Stella told him.

Luke shook against her. "What's wrong? You're scaring me. We're fine. I know we were a little late, but you could have called—oh right, my cell isn't working," she said. She would have to have it replaced next time she was in town.

"No, and Stella didn't answer hers, either," Brycen said with a bit of a reproach in his voice.

"I forgot to grab it on my way out. I'm sorry to have worried you."

"Shit. Babe, please promise me you'll bring it with you from now on. I can't go through this again. My heart can't take it." Brycen told Stella, his voice thicker than usual.

Luke had yet to release her. He took deep breaths, and when he finally was able to pull away from her, he gave her a soft kiss. "Let's get inside and we'll fill you in on what's going on."

They hadn't even sat in the living room when Jace rushed in. "Thank, fuck," he said. His steps took him past her, then she heard a little squeak coming from Stella.

"I missed you too, but I can't breathe, Jace," she said.

"Where the hell have you two been? Why weren't you answering your phone?" Jace came toward her. "And that goes for you too, Maddie. You're important to Luke, so you're important to all of us. You can't disappear like that. It's not safe."

The next thing she knew, Jace gave her a huge hug too. Wow, whatever was going on, it was serious to have shaken these big, fierce men.

"Jace, they're okay. They don't know what's been going on. Let's get them caught up. When everything settles down again, I'll get Maddie a new phone. Until then, if they go anywhere, they'll have to be accompanied."

***

Luke hadn't restricted her before. She wouldn't like it, but her safety had to come first. He hoped she would understand, but he wasn't ready to compromise on that one.

"Please, we're safe at home. Tell us what's happened." She sat on the couch, and Luke sat with her, pulling her into his side. Any separation from her at that point was more than he, or his dragon, could handle.

"I'm going to go down and get the men to come back. I'm glad you're both okay," Jace said, before he left.

"Where are the other men?" Stella asked.

Luke took a steadying breath. "After you left, we had some company. Three men. A man claiming to be Maddison's boyfriend, and two police officers came up here demanding to speak with her."

Maddie gasped. "I don't have a boyfriend. Well, I didn't up until a couple of days ago," she protested, and his heart did a little flip. She saw them as a couple, which was great because he would never be able to let her go. If he had his way, she wouldn't move back to the village at all, even when it was safe again.

"I know, love," he told her. "I could smell the lie for what it was, but that wasn't all. After we denied them entry and demanded a warrant, they got angry. We suspect they're hunters, but no one threatened us or attacked, so our hands were tied. It wasn't until they were about to leave that one of the officers got a message through his radio. The last thing he said before they peeled out of here was that they'd found you in the village and that there would be no little dragons in the area anytime soon." Another shudder shook him, and he pulled Maddie closer still. If he thought she'd tolerate it, he'd pull her onto his lap to hold her, or better yet, drag her upstairs and keep her locked up until everything blew over.

"Crap. I'm sorry, babe." Stella said. "You must have been worried sick. I promise no one bothered us while we were down there. They probably said that to rile you up. Had you attacked, they could have hauled you in. You would have been killed without a trial."

Maddie stiffened and she turned her head in his direction. "Is that true? Could they do that to you?"

"They could, which is why we had to stay behind. Do you have any idea how hard that was? Sending other men out looking for our mates? I may never let you go out without me again," he joked. Now that she was safe, he could breathe again, but the fear of losing her had cemented a few things home. One, he was already so in love with his mate, that he wouldn't survive if she denied his claim, and two, he'd do whatever it took to have her agree to become his. And the sooner, the better. As each of the men came home, they checked in on the women, their relief so obvious it was almost funny. Each of them had similar messages... never scare them like that again, and Luke wholeheartedly agreed.

For the first time in ages, they all ate together. No one willing to leave the women unprotected, even though there were home and as safe as anyone could ever be. After they had eaten, a few of the men went to put the tree on the stand, while others brought boxes of ornaments down. By the time the tree was decorated, the men were happier, more settled, and started trickling back to their own quarters.

"You almost ready for bed?" he asked Maddie. He was more than ready to have some time alone with his mate. He needed to touch her and be with her in every way. It would soothe both him, and the dragon, like nothing else could.

She stretched and stood. "I am." She folded up her walking stick, and held her hand out for him to take.

"Good night," he told the others as he led her out the door.

"Maybe tomorrow you can tell me what the tree looks like. I've never seen one, but my mother used to describe it to me when I was a child."

"Maybe you'll get to see one for yourself someday," he told her. He hadn't mentioned this to her yet, but with the dragon's healing abilities, it wasn't out of the realm of possibility that she might benefit from their mating, and if it helped her make her decision to be mated easier, then he'd take it.

"No. It's impossible. I've seen every specialist out there," she said as they entered the bedroom. Before he could say anything more, Maddie released his hand, grabbed a package from the bed, and headed for the bathroom. She turned only enough for him to see her nibbling on her lip. "I'll be right back. You might want to take some of your clothes off, I want to give you your Christmas present a little early," she said, before disappearing into the washroom and closing the door.

« CHAPTER 13 »

Maddie freshened up before putting on the sexy blue negligee Stella had helped her pick, promising it was his favorite color. It clung to her curves just right, and when she slid her fingers around the silky edge of material covering her breasts, she found a generous amount of cleavage exposed. Perfect. Never in a million years had she thought she would tie herself to a man after having only known him for a couple of days, but that was exactly what she was doing. And what was worse, she had no doubts that it was what she wanted and needed most.

She took a moment to brush her hair out, letting it fall in soft waves around her shoulders, then finally went back to the bedroom.

The moment she came in, his sexy growl filled the room. She made herself walk slowly, wanting him to watch her as she came for him. She was a woman on a mission, and by the end of the night, he would be hers.

"You look stunning," he told her. Sitting on the edge of the bed as he was, his head was at the perfect height, so when he leaned forward, he placed a soft kiss to each mound of her breasts, but as much as she enjoyed it, she wouldn't be sidetracked.

"Did you take all your clothes off?" she asked. Before he had the chance to answer, she placed her palms on his chest and shoved him back, not aggressively, but enough that he knew that she wanted.

"I did."

She climbed over him, straddling his stomach, caressing his chest with the tips of her fingers. Goosebumps rose on his skin, and he sucked in a breath. "Good."

She leaned in, eager for a taste of his lips, but he brought his hands to her belly, and to her breasts. "Mmm... not this time," she said, stopping his exploration by capturing his hands. She brought them down to her hips. "You can touch here, but nowhere else."

He growled again, and Maddie's heart raced a little faster. "Is that right? What happens if I break the rules?"

"Nothing," she smiled down at him, "but I think you'll like it better if you don't."

The boldness of her kiss had his fingers tightening on her hips, but he kept them where they were. She slid her body lower so that his cock poked through between them, hard and ready between her folds.

Luke moaned as she rocked her pelvis against him, taking her pleasure from his body, as she was giving him his. "I won't last long if you keep doing that," he warned, but that was okay. She wanted him to lose control.

She straightened again, giving him plenty of time to take in the sight of her sitting there. When his fingers started moving more restlessly at her hips, she used her own hands, sliding them up her body to her chest. She cupped her breasts, bringing them together, then rolling her nipples between her thumb and finger as he watched. When she rocked her pelvis again, so did he, giving her more contact with his shaft, making them both moan.

"So naughty. Are you certain you want to do that?" she asked as she released her breasts.

"I won't do it again. Please, don't stop," came his husky reply.

She leaned forward, licking and nipping at the hard muscle covering the right side of his chest. His cock twitched beneath her. With everything she was doing, her own need climbed higher and higher. She wanted to position him and sink onto his cock, but that would have to wait. She needed to draw out the dragon. She circled her tongue around his nipple, pulled back, and blew on it, then when he moaned, flicked her tongue over it, catching the small ring there and flipping it to the other side with her tongue.

Her fingers found the other, and she fondled it, stroking all around it before giving it a gentle tug. He loved when she played with his nipples, and she was more than happy to use them to her advantage.

When she sat astride him again, she reached down and lifted the hem of her negligee, revealing her body to him inch by slow inch. She tossed it to the side and arched her back. His eyes were on her, and her nipples pebbled, knowing he was looking at her while she took her time loving his body. When she lifted her hands to her breasts again, he growled. Not the soft, sexy growl from before, but a more assertive, dominant one, one that told her that he was losing the battle with the dragon. She bit her bottom lip, trying to conceal her smile.

Arching her back, she gave both nipples a tweak, following it with a moan as pleasure flooded her. "Do you know what I want, Luke?" she asked, her head thrown back as she resumed rocking over his cock.

"No, please, tell me," he said, his voice gravelly.

"I want your cock inside me so much it hurts," she said, "but not yet. I want to feel you pounding into me until I can't think, and can't breathe. I want to break into a million pieces as you make me come, but not until I feel your lips on mine, your tongue on my skin, and your teeth, right here," she said as she ran a finger along the base of her neck.

Luke's reaction was instant. The growl from before came back, more forceful. His hands slid up to her waist, but she didn't try to stop him. She wanted him to take control—then to lose it to the dragon. "I want you to bite me again, Luke. Harder than before."

"Maddie," he whispered, his voice hoarse, "you don't know what you're asking. I don't want to scare you."

"Oh, I know what I'm asking. Make me yours. I want your mate's bite. I need to feel your teeth sinking into my skin—"

With a strength greater than any man should possess, he lifted her from his body and spun her around. One moment she was straddling him, the next she was on hands and knees before him. His hands were on her hips again, and the head of his cock nudged at her entrance.

"Are you sure, Maddison? There's no turning back once it's done," he warned, but even as he spoke, he slid into her slowly, letting her feel every hard inch of him.

"Yes, like that," she whispered as she shoved her hips back, taking him when he didn't quite move fast enough.

"Don't be afraid, it won't hurt you," he told her as he thrust into her, filling her.

"I'm not afraid. I want the dragon to come forward. I want your claim, Luke." She pulled her hair to the side, revealing her neck.

***

Luke had been fighting an upward battle to keep the dragon at bay while she'd put herself on display for him while teasing his cock with her warm, moist flesh. But when she told him what she needed, and what she wanted, even though he knew he had lost, he had maintained some level of control. It wasn't until she bared her neck and told him she wanted to be his, that his tenuous grip on self-restraint disappeared.

His jaw ached, and he knew it was only a matter of time before his teeth sharpened in preparation for the bite. Her soft moans and whimpers only added fuel to his already raging desire. Each time he looked down at the delicate line of her back, the soft curve of her neck, the pulse in his cock throbbed harder until he couldn't stop. He grabbed a handful of her hair, then wrapped his free hand around her chest, pulling her upright so that her back was against his chest. It meant shallower thrusts, but gave him better access to her body.

He brought his lips to her shoulder, tempting the dragon beyond reason, then moved to nuzzle her ear. "Is this what you want, baby?" he asked, his voice deeper, more guttural than ever. With his free hand, he skimmed her waist, then dipped lower to slide between her folds.

He wasn't going to last much longer, but he wanted her in the middle of her orgasm before he bit her. He circled the little nub, the rough pad of his finger slipping around and around. With each tiny stroke, she moaned louder and louder.

He tugged on her hair, tilting her head to the side before he brought his mouth to her neck. Tracing his tongue along the length of it was both torture and sweet, sensual pleasure. Soon, he'd have his mark there, but not yet.

Maddie jerked in his arms, as his finger made another rotation, and he thrust into her again. With each little circle, he went harder, faster. Her moans and whimpers grew louder. She tried to move, to bring her head upright again, but he wouldn't let her.

Little tremors pulsed around his cock, and he knew she was close. Without warning, he pulled his finger from her clit, waited for a second, then gave it a few little slaps in rapid succession. Maddie held her breath, then let out a long moan as he slid his finger around her clit again.

"Do you like that? Want me to do it again?" he asked.

Maddie didn't even try to answer, nodding her head, what little she could in the position she was in, instead.

He pulled his hand back again, and she held her breath, waiting. Five little slaps, harder than before, and she cried out. When his finger found her again, she jerked in his arms. The muscles encasing his cock trembled and tightened. He flicked her clit harder. His gums burned as the points of his teeth broke through. Already his mouth watered. He thrust faster, sliding all the way in, retreating, then slamming in again. When she cried out, her body squeezing with all the power inside her, he leaned in and sank his teeth into her flesh.

There was a moment of silence, and then her cries grew louder, more desperate. He pounded into her as she rode the crest of her orgasm, not stopping until he emptied himself inside her, only then was he finally able to release her neck, and bring her down to the mattress. He followed her, pulling her to his chest, nuzzling the spot he'd bitten.

"Are you okay?" he asked when he was able to speak again.

She turned in his arms, her smile serene, and her eyes a little moist. "I'm more than okay," she said as she snuggled into him and closed her eyes, "I'm *mated*."

He had a million questions he wanted to ask her, so many things he wanted to say, but they could wait. She was right, they were mated. He'd have all the time in the world to ask her whatever he wanted. When she woke, he would tell her about the possibility of her gaining her sight if they ever decided to have children.

The very thought of having little dragon children in their clan had him smiling from ear to ear. His entire life had changed in a matter of days, and he was happier than he had ever been, all because of the human woman lying in his arms. First, they had to deal with the hunters taking residence in Glen Farley, then maybe they could start a family.

"You're thinking way too hard. Get some sleep. You'll need your energy when I wake up again, mate," she teased.

"Maddie," he said. "I love you."

She smiled up at him, leaning in for a soft kiss. "I love you, too."

Follow Élianne Adams

For the most up to date information about new releases subscribe to my Newsletter.

Online: www.elianneadams.com
On Facebook: Élianne Adams
On Twitter: @ÉlianneAdams

I love to hear from readers. If you enjoyed Lost in Magic, please leave a review at Amazon.com or Goodreads.com. Your feedback is invaluable to make the stories what they are.

Élianne Adams

http://elianneadams.com/

About the Author

Born of snow and ice, or at least near snow and ice in North Eastern Ontario, Canada, Élianne Adams has always enjoyed curling up with a good book and a warm blanket. Even before she really knew what love was, she dreamed of writing her own happily ever after stories. It wasn't until her very own hero encouraged her to follow her lifelong dream that she began putting the words begging to be told onto the page. When she isn't reading or writing, Élianne can be found spending time with her husband, three children and pets.